ADVANC

FL

A NOVEL

BY JIM MILLER

"This remarkable novel is nothing less than a secret history of California—a radical past that might yet redeem our future."
—Mike Davis, author of *City of Quartz*

❧

"*Flash* is about the search for a usable past in a time and place where, as in Orson Welles's *Touch of Evil*, the future has been all used up—or gentrified. Miller's historical sense is rich and particular, showing a Pynchonesque flair for secret history, and a comparable tenderness for the lost lineages and resilient utopianism of the permanent left."
—David Reid, editor of *Sex, Death, and God in LA*

❧

"If Howard Zinn had written a novel about the I.W.W. in border country during the Mexican revolution, one that was also a family saga and a mystery revealing the secret history of the twentieth century, it would read like *Flash*, which deals in the rarest of commodities: hope for our future."
—Forrest Hylton, author of *Evil Hour in Colombia*

FLASH

❧ A NOVEL ❧

Flash: A Novel
By Jim Miller

© 2010 Jim Miller

This edition © 2010 AK Press (Edinburgh, Oakland, Baltimore)

ISBN-13: 9781849350259
Library of Congress Control Number: 2010925759

AK Press   AK Press UK
674-A 23rd Street   PO Box 12766
Oakland, CA 94612   Edinburgh EH8 9YE
USA   Scotland
www.akpress.org   www.akuk.com
akpress@akpress.org   ak@akdin.demon.co.uk

The above addresses would be delighted to provide you with the latest AK
Press distribution catalog, which features several thousand books, pamphlets,
zines, audio and video recordings, and gear, all published or distributed by AK
Press. Alternately, visit our websites to browse the catalog and find out
the latest news from the world of anarchist publishing:
www.akpress.org | www.akuk.com
revolutionbythebook.akpress.org

Printed in Canada on 100% recycled, acid-free paper with union labor.

Cover by Chris Wright | Interior by Kate Khatib

FLASH

❧ A NOVEL ❧

BY JIM MILLER

AK PRESS

EDINBURGH • OAKLAND • BALTIMORE

1

WANTED

FOR GRAND LARCENY.

BOBBY FLASH

Nativity, American; 25 years old; height 5 ft. 4 inches; weight 150 pounds; brown hair; smooth shaven; light complexion; occupation dish washer, harvest stiff, bricklayer, etc.; two gold upper front teeth; corduroy pants, brown corduroy hat; tan button shoes, blue shirt. Member I.W.W., Holtville, Cal. Was under Stanley at Mexicali and under Price at Tia Juana-Mexican Revolution. Left here in the company of Gus Blanco. He was with the I.W.W. bunch that took four horses from Holtville and was mixed up in the robbery at Coyote Well on the night of December 24th, 1911. He is a bad man. I hold warrant for his arrest.

Arrest, hold, and notify,
Mobley Meadows, Sheriff
Imperial Valley, Calif.
Dated: El Centro, Cal.,
January 2d, 1912

Who was Bobby Flash? I copied down the information and put the yellowed Wanted poster back in the folder. The next piece in the file was a mug shot of a young man staring hard into the camera with a defiant half smile that revealed what appeared to be a gold tooth. I looked at his face, under a mop of short but shaggy brown hair. His gaze was piercing and he had a fresh-looking scar under his left eye. I noticed that his work shirt was unbuttoned at the top and his overalls hung higher on his right shoulder than his left. On the back of the photo someone had written

"Buckshot Jack, San Diego 1912," but that had been crossed out by a different hand and replaced with "Bobby Flash, San Diego 1912?" I smiled at the thought of myself, Jack Wilson, being tagged with the nickname "Buckshot," but I was more intrigued by the correction. Was this really Bobby Flash? I stopped for a moment, lost in thought. What drew me to him? Perhaps it was the vague stories about my "crazy commie great grandfather" that my mom would toss off when she was assailing my father's side of the family. They had always resonated with me—just not in the way she had intended. And, perhaps it was just a flight of fancy, but I thought Flash looked a bit like my son Hank thrust back in time (minus the gold tooth). OK. Enough already. Maybe it was just the name, Flash.

I checked the time. It was 4:30. I looked up and saw that the librarian was still occupied at the front desk so I continued to inspect the file. The next piece was another Wanted poster:

WANTED

FOR GRAND LARCENY AND ROBBERY.

GUS BLANCO OR BUNCO

Nativity, American; age 30; height 5 ft. 8 in.; weight 157 pounds; brown hair; no beard; small moustache; gray eyes; chunky nose; red cheeks; occupation bronco buster and cow puncher; slightly stooped shoulders, upper lip hangs over lower, walks like a man stove up from riding horses; left here wearing blue overalls and black felt hat. Is a member of I.W.W. [agitator], canvasser for Industrial Workers of the World. Was in Mexican Revolution, first under Berthold at Mexicali, and at Alamo under Mosby at Tecate also under Price at Tia Juana in C Troop. Will probably find him around I.W.W. halls and men. He is also in the bunch that took the horses from Holtville and started for San Diego.

He was the leader of the I.W.W. men here and is an all around bad man. Anything you may do to get this man will be very much appreciated. I hold warrant for this man.

Arrest, hold and notify,
Mobley Meadows, Sheriff.
Imperial County, Calif.
Dated: El Centro. Cal.,
January 2d 1912

So Bobby Flash was with Blanco and the Wobblies who flooded into San Diego in 1912, the year of the free speech fight. Except this band appears to have been fleeing after the Mexican army took back Tijuana, and the United States sent in Federal troops to round up the American revolutionaries. Many were killed, hundreds arrested, but somehow Flash and Blanco slipped out of the trap. By March, the I.W.W. would call in an army of thousands of bindlestiffs and professional agitators to join them in the battle for free speech, but it looked like Flash and Blanco were there before the main action started. It had been a blood bath, and I thought a story on the centennial anniversary would be great, but I needed an angle and perhaps these two outlaws would provide it. I looked for another mug shot but, unfortunately, there was no picture of Gus Blanco. What I did find was a picture of the lawman, Mobley Meadows, Imperial County's first sheriff. He didn't fit the mold of a TV western tough guy. Instead, he was a patrician-looking fellow, almost effete—the kind of guy who liked to call people "bad men." Just as I was about to dig through the rest of the file, the librarian, a balding, pudgy, middle-aged man, walked over and told me it was closing time. I managed to talk him into making me a couple of photocopies of the Wanted posters and then headed out of the archives room past a cluster of homeless men outfitted in army surplus and Padres giveaway gear who were lingering by the restroom, waiting to be prodded over to the stairs and out onto the street for the long hard night.

Out on E Street, everything was vivid as it always is after your head has been stuck in a stack of papers for the better part of the afternoon. I stopped and noticed, for the first time, the lantern in the center of a circle of mosaic tiles on the sidewalk in front of the library, and the sailing ship at the heart of the San Diego seal a few steps away. Walking past the stout fellow packing up the coffee cart out front I nearly bumped into a pair of sleek Italian women, language school tourists most likely, on their way to the Gaslamp District. They both had long, lush black hair and were chatting animatedly in their native tongue. One of them threw her head back when she laughed and raised her arms in the air like a conductor. A car rolled by with a Radiohead song blasting and another with radio news. "Today, the markets fell on reports..." was all I heard before it faded into the evening. The sky was dark blue beginning to bleed red as I crossed the street and begged my way past the security guard at the post office door so I could check my mailbox. Once inside, I hustled over to the wall of little copper squares and quickly did my combination to find some junk mail and a letter from my son. I shut the box and stopped for a moment to look up at the ceiling of the beautiful old WPA building. Like the funky fifties library, it is one of San Diego's few remaining nods to history with its simple yet elegant modernist design, the light blue molding framing the ceiling, a long rectangle with a row of lamps lining the center. It was quiet like a church with the crowd gone and I wished I could stay and read Hank's letter there, but the guard was already on his way over to put an end to my reverie.

I put the letter in my back pocket, strolled down E street to

5th Avenue, turned left and walked half a block to where *The New Sun* had just opened up its office on the second floor of the Hubbell Building, above a wine bar. It was a gorgeous late-nineteenth century space—1887, to be precise—that we'd never be able to keep, but it was great for the time being. My boss, Neville, the owner and editor, was a solid guy, a trust-fund radical from a conservative family who was willing to spend a lot of money for a while in order to irritate his family. Once things got close to affecting his personal bottom line it would be over, but, for now, it beat the alternative—unemployment. I had burned all my other bridges in town.

I started back with the *SD Weekly*, a sad imitation of an alternative weekly owned by a pugnacious Christian conservative who reveled in irritating the powers that be as long as they were his personal enemies. He was an ex-Marine who still wore a crew cut. He had a face like a bulldog and sported a bowtie and pants that were always a bit too high. "Sarge," as all the writers called him, could be nice, but he had a mean streak. Thus he loved my pieces exposing land deals that benefited the business elites who had funded the campaigns of half the city council and the mayor. It turns out that this wing of the local Republican Party was at odds with the "values" folks. So I went after the money people. This led to a brand of quixotic muckraking that Sarge thought was perfectly fine until I started going after some of his sacred cows. The piece that got me fired was an exposé on an education reformer who went to the boss' church and turned out to be a convicted pedophile. I called it, "Reform, This." He thought it was "tasteless" and replaced me with a guy who went after the labor unions instead, as the city's only daily, the right-wing *Imperial Sun,* always did.

My next stop was *The Independent*, a former punk rock mag that was trying to compete with the *Weekly*. The editor there,

Billy Zero (he went by his pen name), was a well-meaning but not particularly sharp fellow who thought of himself as the coolest guy in town. Zero answered directly to the corporate office that ran about twenty other "independent" weeklies across the country, but he had a tattoo and a little earring so the alternateens he hired to write rock reviews for nothing thought he was hip. I treaded water there for a few years as a kind of utility infielder doing stuff on culture and politics without much problem. I did a piece on the owner of the *Weekly* and his connections to the Christian right, anti-abortion, and anti-gay rights crusades and Zero loved it. I wrote a column called "Lotusland Blues" for a year and pissed off half the city. Zero loved that, too. Things were looking up—for a while.

What got me in trouble with *The Independent* was a story I did called "Cool Gentrification" about how the last old bars and single-family businesses were getting pushed out of downtown by "hipster capitalists," a few of whom frequently advertised in the paper. That piece led to a chat with Zero over beers at the Barge, the oldest bar in the city, which used to be a haven for fishermen and union factory workers before those industries largely vanished from town. Now the old scrap yard and dingy boat dealerships that had surrounded it had been replaced by high-end condos. Bye bye blue collar, hello hipsters! In any event, Zero bought me a beer, sat down next to me at the bar, ran his hand through his spiky hair, and said, "Jack, I think you are getting too predictable."

"Predictable?" I asked, staring at him as he squirmed a little on his barstool.

"Yeah, Jack, all the 'fuck gentrification' stuff is getting old," he said with a whiff of condescension while refusing to look me in the eye.

"How so?" I queried deadpan, but suspicious. "I thought we were an alternative weekly."

"I don't know," he said trying to look caring as he delivered a dose of what he seemed to think was tough love. "Maybe the alternative to alternative is alternative." He looked down at his tattoo. I laughed once I realized he was serious.

"Zero," I started, unable to help myself, "that's the dumbest fucking thing I've ever heard. You can fire me if you want to, but that's just stone cold stupid bullshit."

"You can be defensive if you want to," he said, assured of his wisdom. "But I think you should be open minded and think about what I said." He got up and left the money for the beer. I stayed and ordered another. Later that night, I got online and did a little research on Zero. I found an article in an industry rag where he said that, "We may come off as more left than thou, but all the while we're busting our asses to please our advertising base." It turns out that the hipster capitalists had flooded the paper with complaints and threatened to pull their ads if the tone of the paper didn't change. If Zero had been straight with me, I might have considered his plight with the corporate office, but his pathetic advice had pissed me off. I decided to write myself out of a job, make him fire me like a good old-fashioned "uncool" boss.

I began by doing a story on the hideous architectural malpractice of one of *The Independent*'s main advertisers. Entitled, "A Sick Joke on the Avant Garde," the piece included pictures of some of their marquee condominiums and mocked their stunningly ugly design. My "Best Of" list included "Best Santa Fe Style Stalinist Block Building," "Best Postmodern Prison Bunker," "Best Retarded Sailboat-Themed Monstrosity," and a special category for "Best Unintentionally Cartoonish Mural Art on a Live/Work Space." They lost the ads. No comment from Zero. One of the alternateens got a TV show about local rock bands on the local FOX News station, and I did a column entitled "OK, Punk Really is Dead Now." Still, I was gainfully employed. Only my final shot, "Alternative, Inc." featuring Billy Zero's quote in the industry mag and a discussion of the parent corporation's other connections, which included lots of unsavory, uncool things like toxic waste dumps and union busting law firms, did the trick.

Eventually *The Independent*'s parent corporation outsourced the local reporting to India, I kid you not. The "reporters" watched the City Council meetings over the internet live and Googled their sources. They even got rid of the underpaid music reporters by holding a weekly contest on the paper's blog called "Concert review of the week," where an unpaid blogger's take on the big show took the place of an underpaid staffer. Album reviews came off the wire. Mercifully, the parent corporation's experiment with outsourcing local news and hip commentary died, and they shut down the paper, but give it time. Oh brave new world with such creatures in it... So anyway, that's how I ended up here at *The New Sun* tossing copies of century-old Wanted posters on Neville's desk.

"Let's find out who Bobby Flash was," I said without any introduction.

Neville picked up the copies and read them studiously, pushing his little round glasses down his nose a bit and nodding slowly. "Do you want to do a quick piece or a feature? And why not Bunco? He was the leader of the group wasn't he?"

"Well, the hundred-year anniversary of the free speech fight is coming up so I think it merits a series." I said, pushing the envelope as always. "And we've got a picture to go with Flash's name. Plus, I'm drawn to bit players. The folks in the background are always more interesting, no?"

"And that's important to you and a handful of people," he said without looking up.

"I'll make it important."

He smiled and looked up slowly. "Start doing it and talk me into it later. In the meantime, I've got a few other things for you, one on something big in Tijuana. The other is local. You can work on Bobby Flash for the long haul." He handed me a folder.

"Fair enough," I said looking over a letter in the folder that Neville had just handed me. It had been written on behalf of the women in a Tijuana neighborhood who lived down the hill from an abandoned maquiladora. When the rains hit, the waste from the plant flowed down into the dirt streets by their homes. Bad things were happening, and nobody was paying any attention. Bobby Flash would have to wait until next week.

I said goodnight to Neville and headed down the stairs out onto 5th Avenue. There were a few couples sipping zin in Vineland just out the door. I headed up toward Broadway to the bus stop, pausing at 5th and E for a moment to try to imagine the soap-boxers stirring it up a century ago. The fancy bar and grill on the corner made the job tough, but I thought for a moment of Bobby Flash hopping up to say, "Fellow workers and friends," before being dragged off by the cops. Or maybe he got into a good little rant before they could grab him: "The Working class and the employing class have nothing in common. There can be no peace as long as hunger and want can be found among millions. How come the bosses got all of the good things? You tell me why." I smiled as a pack of suits strolled by to hit Ostera, a "Watergrill." Crossing E, I made my way past the new restaurant of the week, a pawn shop, a check-cashing place, and the last remaining cheap eats joints before I hit Broadway and just caught the bus that would take me up to Golden Hill where I lived in a flat behind a big old house. I dropped in my fare and walked to the back. In the dirty white light I saw the tired, after-work faces of cashiers, janitors, secretaries, security guards, and the homeless men who rode the line like Bartleby the Scrivener, preferring not to leave until they were kicked off at the end of the route.

Neville never told me what to write or even what the lead was, he just handed things over to me like an old-school newsman in a thirties movie. I loved that about him. I sat down and looked over the other item in the folder he'd given me. It was a copy of an email the paper had received from a Marine at Camp Pendleton whose buddy had shot himself the week before. The local TV news had done the "fallen hero" bit but there was some nasty stuff about his experience in Iraq that nobody had mentioned. The Marine wanted to talk to somebody. I looked up at the reflection of my fellow passengers in the window. Indistinct shapes, blurring together. The bus rolled by Church of Steel Tattoo, Chee Chee, El Dorado, and a block that had been leveled for redevelopment. Just then I remembered my son's letter in my back pocket. I took it out and read:

Dad,

Just have a few minutes to get this out before work. Things are going OK with my classes but none of them are very interesting. Other than the job thing it's hard to see the point. English is boring, math tedious, and political science lame. I'll try to stick it out as you advise but other than the "better job" thing there's not much I'm learning that I couldn't learn on my own. I know you said not to follow your example, but you never finished school and you have a job, right? Not giving up yet, I'm just saying I think you did all right, no matter what that asshole Kurt says. Maybe it's just having to stay in that house to save money. Shit, I'm in my twenties! Mom and Kurt are fighting all the time and it gets me down having to listen. Sorry to dump all this on you, but I know you'll understand. I'll be OK. Off to serve coffee to the masses.

Love, Hank

P.S. How 'bout a visit sometime? Or me down in SD?

I smiled, shook my head, folded the letter up carefully, and put it back into the envelope and then in my back pocket. Hank always sent his letters to the PO box since I moved a lot. He and a few select friends were are the only people who have that address other than the junk mail people who seem to be able to ferret you out no matter where you try to hide. I insist on letter writing; it's my nod to a dying art and the notion that fast isn't always better.

The bus was lurching up the hill toward my stop and I stared out the window into the night at the lights in the front windows of apartments and houses—strangers doused in the dull glow of TVs or sitting down for an evening drink. I got off the bus when it hit 25th, to head to my flat. On the way there I nodded to the doorman smoking outside the Turf Club and glanced through the window at a few solitary faces staring at laptop screens in the Krakatoa Café. I lived behind a Victorian house that the owner had chopped into four claustrophobically small units. My place had a postage-stamp lawn and little porch outside the studio. I had made it—I was in my forties and still doing the work I did when I was in my twenties. And my kid seemed bent on replicating my mistakes. If my mom's stories about my "hobo" ancestor were correct, maybe it was in the genes.

Long ago I had been relegated to weekend visits, so I was the "cool dad." It was true, Hank's stepfather Kurt *was* an asshole, but unfortunately that seemed to be sending Hank the message that people who could support themselves adequately were *all* assholes. Partially true perhaps, but a dangerous generalization. Trisha, Hank's mother, had left me back when he was a baby. I had been working for the *LA Scene*, an upstart alternative weekly in the days before they were all bought up by media corporations. Anyway, I had been out covering a Jane's Addiction show at the Howl club down by McArthur Park and came home to an empty apartment and a note: "Sorry Jack, I can't do this anymore." By "this" Trisha meant living on my shit wages with a baby. She had been a hairdresser, but quit when she got pregnant, to my surprise, apparently expecting that fatherhood would transform me into a proper provider so she could stay at home. Instead, she got a live-in boyfriend who had to leave her alone at home a lot so he could bring back an inadequate paycheck.

We'd been living in a cheap apartment in the San Fernando Valley with a banner perpetually strung on the side of the building, which read "Move In Now!" Perhaps the owner thought he needed to advertise endlessly because the combination of the 24/7 smell of greasy chili burgers emanating from the Tommy's next door and the pungent odor of late night hops from the Anheiser Busch Brewery across the street drove everyone who could afford to leave out of the complex. None of our neighbors spoke English, a fact that Trisha frequently commented on, along with the 5:00 AM Norteño music that the neighbors blasted from their pickups as they took off for work. "It's a hard life," I'd tell her.

After she left, she moved in with her mother, who consistently referred to me as "the loser" during my son's formative years. This made for a painful and ambivalent childhood for Hank. Nonetheless, the harder Trish and her Mom tried to push him away from me, the more he pulled his way back. Even as a very young boy Hank would draw pictures of "Daddy at a music show" or

"Daddy writing." It drove them fucking crazy and I loved him for it.

A couple of years after Trisha moved out, she hooked up with Kurt, an ex-frat boy from USC who had a job in real estate. They got married and Kurt set about ruining Trisha's life in a whole new way. He had affairs, berated her in front of Hank, and dissed me constantly. Kurt was an all-star. His saving grace: money. Hence Trisha was long-suffering and materially comfortable in West LA.

Trisha and I met back in 1987 at Al's Bar, the legendary punk spot in the loft district of downtown LA where a lot of artists lived. It was walking distance from the Atomic Café on the edge of Little Tokyo. I loved Al's, both for the good music and for the fact that it was a place where Bukowski used to drink. The neon sign behind the bar said, "Tip or Die." I was there that night to cover a tiny theater troupe's version of Kerouac's *Tristessa*. They put the show on in the alley behind the bar and an audience of a dozen or so people sat on the same kind of metal bleachers they have at little league fields. It was a dramatic adaptation of the Kerouac novel about Jack and his friends in Mexico City, and Jack's brief dalliance with a soulful, tragically beautiful prostitute, whose name means "sadness." The actors entered stage right from the back door of the bar and did a decent job of invoking the beat mood with no set, no costumes, and no music. Spare, earnest, and bittersweet. My review was entitled, "Beat in the Alley."

I remember spending a lot of time during the play staring up at a high rise framed by the narrow alley and glancing over at Trisha. She was dressed in all black (a sort of uniform then) with long hair dyed bright red. Her eyes were blue-green and she had a sweet smile that lit up her face. After the play, we both stayed to listen to a cowpunk band from Austin, Texas, named Hillbilly

Tryst or something like that. I bought her a beer and we talked about the play, about the Beats, about music. We agreed that life was tragic. She let her friends go home and left with me, strolling down the dark street lined with sleeping bodies under dirty blankets or flattened cardboard boxes. When we got to my car I kissed her softly and gazed into her alabaster face. We looked up at the crescent moon above the looming skyline. The whole city was mine, the big wide world. I was in love. We went home together, and it was all good, for quite a while.

Back then, Trisha rented a room in a big house up in the Hollywood hills from the guy who ran The Grave on Hollywood Boulevard. Actually she chipped in for his rent. The place was really owned by a nearly senile old woman in the valley who lived there when she was a kid. She hadn't done her homework, and Zane, the Ghoul, and Trisha were getting the whole two-story house with its nice yard overlooking a canyon and a view of the Hollywood sign for a mere pittance. Zane, who managed the club at night, had a day job with the Water and Power Company so he more or less had his shit together. The Ghoul, on the other hand, played in a local band called Night of the Living Dead and was a full-on junkie.

By this time in my youth, I had grown my shaggy hair out to about shoulder length and usually never wore anything fancier than jeans, a t-shirt, and black converse sneakers. Trisha used to make fun of my lack of fashion sense. That said, the Ghoul, who rarely bathed, never washed his clothes, and made little effort to conceal his track marks, made me look like a *GQ* cover boy. He usually lounged around the basement room in a leather jacket with no shirt underneath and boxer shorts. When I came over Trisha and I would do everything we could to avoid being drawn down into his lair. Suffice to say we never chased the dragon.

The rest of the place was fantastic. Zane, a manic Aussie with a thick mane of long red hair, had an impressive collection of Marilyn Monroe photos that lined the hallways upstairs: Marilyn in *Playboy*, Marilyn in *Bus Stop*, Marilyn pouting, Marilyn teasing, Marilyn tragic and innocent, Marilyn in death. He and his girl-friend, Cat—an aspiring actress who had her own place but basically lived with Zane—had filled the living room with vintage furniture carefully selected from stores on Melrose—late-fifties and early-sixties Moderne. The end tables of the leopard-skin couch were littered with copies of *Screw*, *The Hollywood Reporter*, and *BAM*.

Trisha worked on Melrose in a salon called the Union Jack, which the owner had decorated with British rock posters, Sex Pistols, Clash, The Who, etc. Whenever I could, we'd meet for lunch or for drinks after work. We scoured used-record stores for hidden gems, had lots of coffee, and looked through second-hand shops. During that period, Trisha never said a thing about money. We just talked and made love and went out to see music. She read a lot so we rapped about books mostly. We'd both started and then stopped college and figured we didn't need to pay somebody to tell us what to read. She liked the Beats, but also Anaïs Nin, Virginia Woolf, and Sylvia Plath. Thus the talk had a lot to do with sex and death and suffering and angst and *carpe diem*. One thing Trisha didn't share with me was an interest in politics. I just assumed we were in tune at a basic level.

Sometimes we'd go downtown between the Nickel and the Garment District to Gorky's on open mic night to listen to bad poetry for laughs. Gorky's was a hip Russian-themed cafeteria that served borscht, brewed their own beer, and had music, art, and poetry every week. Before I met Trisha, I had a brief flirtation with poetry. I read a lot of Bukowski and wrote a few pieces about waking up with a bad hangover and hating the world. When I went to my first open mic night at Gorky's I discovered that everyone else had read a lot of Bukowski and had a lot of hangovers. We all sucked. After that realization, I still liked to go to Gorky's, but solely for amusement. One night, Trisha and I almost bust a gut laughing after an English grad student from USC read a poem about a roach crawling on her IUD. The woman wasn't pleased with our response and flipped us off. Of course, this only made us laugh all the more.

Sometimes there would be surprises though. One evening, after a series of poets who overcame their lack of skill with the language by yelling at the top of their lungs, a petite young woman in an X t-shirt nervously came to the mic and read an elegy called "Anonymous" about a man who died on the street outside her loft downtown. It was a cry for those who die unknown in solitary rooms, a howl for the utterly forlorn. It was so stark and beautiful after what had preceded it that quite a few people, myself included, were moved to tears. It was beyond irony, for once.

I was pretty busy then with the *LA Scene*. I did a whole series on the culture of the homeless men who lived by the Los Angeles River. I spent a week sleeping under bridges and hanging out in homeless camps interviewing men around bonfires. One group I found was a band of scavengers. They sold scrap metal on the black market so they'd rip it off of anything they could find and bring it in to the yards. It was a good enough gig to get some of the guys out of the camps and into hotel rooms in the Nickel. Some, though, thought that rent was a waste of coin and preferred to live alfresco. I remember one night in particular. It was February during a cold snap and I was sitting by a fire under a freeway bridge sharing a few bottles of wine and cheap whiskey with twenty men. There was a kind of code in the camps that reminded me of those scenes in *The Grapes of Wrath* where folks on the road would help each other out sometimes. Some of the veterans remembered the old days too. That disappeared when crack hit the scene and people started killing each other for pocket change. A few months after my series, the *LA Times* did a similar thing, but I never got a call or a credit from anybody.

Speaking of crack, I also did a story on the "Contra Cocaine" posters put up all over the city by guerilla poster artist Robbie Conal. The poster featured a skull in the tradition of the *calaveras* in Mexican Day of the Dead art, but this one was wearing a pinstriped suit with a camouflage background. The heading provocatively made the connection between the Reagan Administration's support of the contra insurgency against the Sandinistas in Nicaragua with the little known fact that the contras were flying coke into the US with the help of the CIA. Overnight, 10,000 of these posters went up all over the city, from the alley near my studio apartment in Venice to telephone poles and other public spaces in LA and in seventeen different American cities. I got a photographer to take some greats shots of the posters in Skid Row downtown and interviewed Conal and a local professor at UCLA about the significance of the gesture. The CIA-funded drug runs during the explosion of street gang warfare in LA was strong stuff and despite CIA denials, it turned out to be true. I followed up that story with a piece about Salvadoran death squads chasing down and murdering leftist refugees in Los Angeles. One of my sources got killed before the article went to press. It was one of those epiphanic moments in my life when I realized that anything, no matter how menacing, was possible.

So I was completely immersed in my life as an underpaid jack-of-all-trades, if you'll pardon the pun, for the *LA Scene*, not paying much heed to the future. When I wasn't crashing at Trisha's house in the Hills, she was staying with me at my studio in Venice. We took walks by the canals to feed the ducks and bemoaned each time a McMansion took the place of a cottage. We strolled down the boardwalk on lazy afternoons watching the fire jugglers, listening to pitches from religious cranks, and stopping to be serenaded by troubadours on roller skates. We'd buy books in Small World, and read over beers until sunset. The only bad thing that went down during that period happened back at Trisha's place, when a friend of the Ghoul's OD'd in the bathtub during one of the gatherings in what was an endless stream of house parties. There were tons of people there, and when Zane discovered the body he cleared the house, screaming at everyone to "get the fuck out" and insisting that the Ghoul and his buddies drag the guy's body out of the house. I almost got in a fight trying to persuade them to call an ambulance. Trisha packed up her stuff that night and moved in with me. Within a month she was pregnant.

To be honest I was surprised she wanted to keep the baby. I had told her that it was her body and I'd be there either way. She thought about it and decided to have the kid. "Because I love you," she said. As you might expect, I was scared shitless at the prospect, but soldiered on. Trisha quit her job, and we moved to the Valley to be near my mom's house, as Trisha's family was not too keen on the idea of her having a kid "out of wedlock." I was surprised people still talked that way. In my eyes, Trisha just got more and more beautiful when she was pregnant. She let her hair, naturally black, grow out, and she was radiant. I would write up my pieces and go get her snacks when she needed them. I was with her in the hospital and got up at night to feed little Henry (named after Henry Miller and the "Hank" character in the Bukowski stories).

During this period, there was never any discussion of Trisha being unhappy. Quite the contrary—I remember getting up to feed Hank (Trisha pumped breast milk in bottles so I could do some late night duty), and I walked with him cradled in my arms out onto the steps in front of our place. Despite myself, I got lost in the wonder of my baby boy. The fragility, the improbability of life. I could smell the hops cooking across the way and it was deep and sweet in the hot summer air. At that moment I swore that I'd try to be there for him for the rest of my life. Trisha came out and kissed me on the cheek and we looked at the moon. I'd never felt more love or more peace than in the ocean of it that subsumed me at that moment.

The next night, I drove over the hill to cover the Jane's show at the Howl. I wandered around the gorgeous hotel lobby, went into a room taken over by dozens of huge screens featuring a Burroughs-like cut-up of random black and white stills, some of iconic images like Robert Frank, others looked like family photos, then some blurry color footage from a handheld camera. It lost my attention and I went over to the bar and bought a vodka soda. In the next room, some guy dressed up like Jesus, with a big cross strapped to his back, was crawling around on all fours begging for a gin and tonic. This got old fast so I walked back out to the top of the big staircase in the lobby. It was an elegant setting, a fitting backdrop for Mae West in her prime. By now it was littered with tall, sexy girls, posing by the railing, practicing various stages of ennui. A few looked high on H. They were the kind of women who never gave me the time of day and I was out of the game now anyway.

Jane's Addiction played in another big room that looked as if it had once been the hotel's chapel. The crowd was jammed in tight, flesh against flesh. You could feel the rush of anticipation surge through the room when the band came on stage. They opened with a hard driving version of "Pigs in Zen" and Perry Farrell was in top form, prancing around the stage theatrically and leaping in the air. Everybody went nuts for "Jane Says," but I preferred their cover of the Stones' "Sympathy for the Devil" and the way Farrell's voice poured out longing when they closed with "I Would For You." It made me think of Trisha, and I just wanted to get home. I walked out past the lounging and posing and desiring crowd to my beat-up Mustang. I popped in a Los Lobos tape and glanced up at the downtown skyline as "One Time One Night" came on, and I rolled onto the freeway to head back to the Valley. When I got home, I found the note in our empty apartment. It was a warm summer night and the thick smell of hops and hamburgers made me want to throw up.

2

I showed up at *The New Sun* early in the AM to call my contacts. Neville was already there, working on a review of a string quartet that'd opened a new classical music festival in La Jolla. His politics were very left, but he had a Ph.D. in the Humanities and was extremely well-versed in the arts, opera, and classical music. This was a huge boon for our anemic advertising budget, since we had the best coverage in town and that gave us some cultured readership, which appealed to a handful of advertisers for galleries, wine shops, record stores, travel agents, etc. So the wine and cheese crowd and "adult industry" (porn is the evil twin of every good muckraking weekly) kept Neville's trust fund from being pillaged. Neville ignored my warm greeting, so I left him to his work and poured myself a cup of his coffee before hitting the phone. I had to leave a message for the Marine, but got a hold of Ricardo Flores right away. Ricardo was the spokesman for a coalition of labor and human rights groups. Las Madres Unidas, the women from the neighborhood downhill from the maquiladora, was part of Justicia para Trabajadores, the larger group that he helped run. Ricardo would meet me just over the border at 4:00 if I could make it. I could. It was still early so, with no word yet from the Marine, I decided to go back to the library to finish looking over the I.W.W. file I had been pulled away from yesterday evening. I had Bobby Flash on my mind despite my other obligations. Neville ignored me when I waved to him on the way out.

Back at the archives, I asked the librarian, the same pudgy guy, for a file on the free-speech fight and he brought it over to me glumly. Mostly, it was a fairly haphazard selection of newspaper clippings from 1911 and 1912. I read a pair of dueling rants: The

Union editorialized in favor of the vigilante attacks on the Wobblies and their supporters, while *The San Diego Sun* attacked the owner and editor of the *Union*, John D. Spreckels. One of the attacks was entitled, "Put This in Your Pipe and Smoke it Mr. Anti-Labor Man." In it, the writer decried the way Spreckels sought to run San Diego like General Otis of the *LA Times* had run Los Angeles—as a petty dictator. More to the point, *The Sun* argued, it was clear that Spreckels was most upset about being taxed for "occupying the streets with his railways." I took a few notes and remembered having read that one of the key things that preceded the free speech fight was the effort of the tiny San Diego I.W.W. Local 13, which had only fifty members, to organize the Mexican workers on Spreckels' street car lines.

Unlike the local AFL unions who wouldn't even try to organize Mexicans, blacks, or Chinese workers, the Wobblies welcomed everyone—even unskilled migrant workers. The Wobblies were the only American union to oppose exclusion laws and organize Asians and other workers like the Jews, Catholics, and recent immigrants frequently ignored by the American Federation of Labor. The Industrial Workers of the World was born out of the fires of Colorado mining wars, and the Wobblies thought of themselves as revolutionaries. They rejected contracts, believed in direct action, were suspicious of political organizations, and mixed anarchism, syndicalism, Marxism, and an inverted form of Social Darwinism freely as their rough and ready membership thought of theoretical distinctions as useless nitpicking. (Having covered my share of endless leftist political gatherings, a hostility to useless nitpicking was a sentiment I could get behind.) Believing in "One Big Union of All the Workers," they thought that their form of organizing would eventually lead to a huge general strike in which the workers would take control of the means of production and end the rule of the bosses. They were forming the structure of a new society in the shell of the old. Unrealistic, as it turned out, but a good thought. In San Diego, by hitting Spreckels's streetcar franchise they went straight after the interests of the richest man in town and scared the shit out of the powers that be. I liked that.

For the Wobblies, the whole street-speaking thing was more about organizing than it was about some abstract idea of the Bill of Rights. By standing on a soapbox in the middle of the street they could reach out to the floating unemployed population, disgruntled workers, and others receptive to their message, and educate them about the interests of all workers or agitate them to join a given fight. The goal was to turn those on the outskirts of society away from shame and defeat, and toward anger. They wanted to turn "bums into men." I looked at a picture of a scruffy crowd listening to a soapboxer at 5th and E, and smiled as I imagined the present day parade of bistros, wine-bars, and trendy meat markets. When I had first visited San Diego back in the eighties, downtown had still been a sailor town of dive bars, strip joints, porno shops, greasy spoons, flop houses, and mom and pop shops. Back at the turn of the century, the Gaslamp was called the Stingeree and 5th and E was Heller's Corner. The Stingeree was where most of the working-class whites, white-ethnic immigrants, Chinese, and Mexicans lived. It was full of shops, saloons, cheap hotels, gambling houses, opium dens, and prostitutes. Middle- and upper-class ladies used to complain about having to pass by the soapboxers and the grimy throng of workingmen and other ill-clad, shabby-looking characters. All in all, it sounded a lot more fun back in the day than it is now—unless you're looking for a bad cover band or an overpriced cheese plate.

What kicked off the events that led to the free speech fight was an incident on January 6th, 1912 in which an off-duty cop and real estate man tried to drive his car straight through a street meeting. The crowd rocked his car and slashed his tires even though the Wobbly speaker warned them that this would just give the police an excuse to break up the meeting, which they did. I have to say that after being almost hit by a car, it might be tough for me to show restraint too. I've been known to flip off a heedless driver or two in my day, but that's beside the point. Anyway, after that, Spreckels and his crew saw their opening and pushed San Diego city authorities to pass an ordinance banning street speaking in basically the entire Stingeree District in February 1912. Of course the ban irritated not only the I.W.W. but also a whole range of other folks including the AFL, Socialists, religious leaders and civil libertarians who formed the California Free Speech League to challenge the ban. The I.W.W.'s response was to flood San Diego with thousands of protesters, and when the first waves of the Wobbly army hit town, city authorities passed a "move-on ordinance" that gave police wide powers to break up street meetings and harass "vagrants."

The Wobblies were pretty disciplined and did everything they could to avoid violence because they knew the cops generally welcomed an excuse to bust heads. San Diego police, however, emboldened by the new laws and egged on by the city's bosses, didn't hold back. They waded into crowds with batons flying and beat prisoners all the way to jail. They used fire hoses to knock protesters off their feet, and filled the jails with Wobblies. In jail, the brutality continued with the murder of sixty-five-year-old Michael Hoey, who was savagely beaten by three cops, kicked in the groin multiple times, and left to die on the cement floor of an overcrowded, rat-infested cell. Outside the pen, they shot another Wobbly named Joseph Mikolasek in front of the I.W.W. headquarters. Still, a tough bunch, the Wobblies didn't get scared off.

They kept flooding into town, packing the jails, and singing until it drove the police crazy. In one article I found a quote where a cop whined, "These people do not belong to any country, no flag, no laws, no Supreme Being. I do not know what to do. I cannot punish them. Listen to them singing all the time, yelling and hollering, and telling the jailors to quit work and join the union. They are worse than animals." Great stuff, I thought.

When police brutality didn't work, the city fathers ended up resorting to vigilante terror. Working at the behest of the elite, most of the vigilantes were scared middle-class merchants, aspiring real estate men, clerks, off-duty cops, and otherwise-respectable thugs who were just looking for blood sport. This reminded me of the stuff that happened with the cops around the time of the LA riots. Some of the elites such as George Marston and *The Sun*'s owner, Scripps, didn't support the I.W.W. but did support the idea of free speech. Most, though, were in line with the reign of terror. As the *Union* editorial put it, "Hanging is none too good for them and they would be much better dead; for they are absolutely useless in the human economy; they are waste material of creation and should be drained off into the sewer of oblivion there to rot in cold obstruction like any other excrement." I think it's safe to say they weren't fucking around. So a vigilante army of about 400 men was formed. They met a trainload of incoming Wobblies and beat and tortured 140 men, making them run the gauntlet before sending them bleeding on their walk back to Los Angeles.

I looked over several reports of Emma Goldman's visit to San Diego. Most people who've ever heard of the free-speech fight also know the story of how Goldman, the famous anarchist, was driven out of San Diego by quite a welcoming committee. Met at the Santa Fe depot by a snarling mob of "ladies" screaming for her blood, Goldman was ushered to the US Grant Hotel where the mayor denied her the opportunity to speak to an angry mob in the park across the street below. While this negotiation was taking place, a crew of thugs kidnapped her lover, Ben Reitman, and drove him out to near the Peñasquitos Ranch to meet a pack of vigilantes who proceeded to make him kiss the flag and sing "The Star Spangled Banner." Think of that the next time you're at a ballgame and I bet you won't sing. They stripped Reitman, viciously beat him, jammed a cane up his bunghole, nearly twisted his balls off, and branded I.W.W. in his ass with a lit cigar. He was then tarred and feathered and sent north on foot. What interested me, however, was not the story of these legendary anarchists, but the unknown stories of those who were lost to history.

I kept skimming through the articles, some of which I'd seen quoted in books, until I came upon a longer piece in *The Sun* about the vigilante attacks on free-speech fighters. It gave the basic details but also featured a few "accounts" by victims of the vigilantes. One in particular caught my interest:

> They took us from the cattle pen in groups of five. I remember looking up at the back of the fellow in front of me. It was covered in manure as they had made us lie in a pile of cattle dung while we waited for our turns. The first of the thugs I caught sight of had on a constable's badge and a white handkerchief tied around his left arm. All of them, it turned out had white handkerchiefs on their arms. Most of our captors had a gun or a rifle in one hand and a club or other such weapon in the other. That is unless they had a bottle of whiskey. This gang of fine men of property and law had all got their courage up by getting good and drunk. All the better to be in high spirits while you're beating unarmed men, I suppose. Well, they pushed, kicked and prodded us along to a spot where they had us each pay our respects to the flag. The kid in front of me, about 17 years old, got smacked in the head with a wagon

spoke and he fell to his knees. Kiss it, you F** Son of a B**, Kiss the G** damn flag, they yelled at him. I could see the blood pouring down his face from a head wound. They had no mercy with him, despite his youth. After he performed their profane ritual, he ran the gauntlet of over a hundred men, each one taking a swing with a club, a bat, or some other weapon. By the end of the line, the kid was crawling through the dirt, leaving a trail of blood behind him.

Next they made Giovanni, "the priest" we used to call him on account of his preaching all the time about non-violence, kiss the flag and sing "The Star Spangled Banner." Get it right you Dago Son of a B***, one of the bigger thugs yelled before kicking the back of his legs to bring him to his knees. For Giovanni, the worst was not the spit on his face after his song was complete, but the first horrible blow he took from a wagon spoke with a big spike driven through the end. Giovanni had failed to get his arms up in time and it pegged him straight in the forehead. He went down with a thud and didn't move. He was kicked and poked with more than a few bats and clubs until one of the sharper wits in the pack of wolves got the idea to drag him away and dump his limp body off to the side. I never heard word of Giovanni after that. Lots of fellas went down that way, with no one to remember 'em.

After Giovanni got dragged away, they took big Jacob, or "the Kike" as they called him. They seemed to take a special liking to beating the Jews, Catholics, and Mexicans in our unfortunate little parade. For Jacob, one of the off-duty men of the law selected a hose filled with gravel and tacks. I heard him scream after the first swing and then I was struck from behind by the butt of a pistol and my knees were taken out by a couple swings of a bat. I guess I was a bit too much of a mess for Old Glory 'cause they quickly pushed me past the flag into the gauntlet with no need of a kiss or a song. Just lucky I guess. I couldn't see well through the blood dripping into my eyes but I stayed low and kept my head covered with my arms as I limped through the gauntlet. There was a whole lot of cursing blending together and stupid yelling about anarchy and godlessness and the lesson I was getting from those pious gentlemen with such brave souls. I remember staggering out the back end of the line and being told that if I ever came back, they'd find a nice spot to bury me on some of their pretty real estate. If I learned a lesson there, though, it was that I was through with non-violence. Poor Giovanni's corpse was a sterner teacher than his pretty words.

As told by I.W.W. agitator, Buckshot Jack

I stopped dead and reread the name, flipped back through the file to the mugshot with the same name. When I asked the librarian who had made the correction and changed the name to Bobby Flash on the back of the picture, he didn't know. He walked back to check with the main archivist. No luck. The file was put together years ago by a librarian who had passed away. I read the rest of the article that included another account of the gauntlet, but no more on Bobby Flash or his partner, Gus Blanco. Still, this was an interesting piece in the puzzle. I thought for a whimsical moment about my mysterious great grandfather and let myself ponder the possibility that this could be him. No way, I thought, pulling myself back to the task, it was far too interesting a story for my sad family.

I had the librarian copy *The Sun* article and looked through the rest of the file. No more leads. When the librarian came back to take the file, he recommended I try the Historical Society in Balboa Park. I thanked him and went down to the stacks to find a book on the Magónista revolt of 1911 that I'd been meaning to read. I grabbed it, checked it out, and left the building.

Outside the library it was a beautiful January day, but I hardly noticed that as I walked toward the trolley to meet Ricardo Flores in Tijuana. I was still stuck in my head, thinking about Bobby Flash. Had he been one of the group of Wobblies who were forced to walk back along the railroad tracks toward Los Angeles? Had he been so badly injured that he been taken to a local hospital? There had been nothing in the article beyond the account of the gauntlet. I was still ruminating when I got to the transit center. I absent-mindedly picked up a copy of the *LA Times* at a news rack and had to run to hop on the trolley to San Ysidro. I found an empty pair of seats by the window and put my satchel with the library book and my notes in it on the seat next to me. I glanced across the aisle at a Mexican woman sitting with her two little boys. They had bags full of souvenirs from the San Diego Zoo.

I looked out the window at a utility box that still had a fading Obama "Hope" poster plastered on it. During the campaign, I had been skeptical about the vagueness of Obama's messianic appeal, just as I had been brought to tears when he spoke on more than one occasion. It was a battle between my middle-aged pessimism and some deep need for, well, hope. I think more than a few people felt that way. The front page of the *Times* had a story about things going badly in Afghanistan, one about more layoffs, another about the latest California budget debacle, and an in-depth piece on rising global instability due to the economic crisis. I couldn't help but think of the parallels between the beginning of the last century and this one: the economic and political polarization, the anger at "the bosses" as the Wobblies would say. Now though, people weren't in the streets, at least not yet. People didn't know who to shoot.

I looked up at a bunch of teenage kids jumping on board in National City. What kind of future would these kids have? It was hard to say. There were dark clouds on the horizon, but some-times it was times like these that made people stand up. At the next stop, a pair of soldiers got on board in their white uniforms complete with hats. They were talking loudly about sex with pros-titutes. I picked up the book on the Magónista revolt and flipped to the middle to look at a black-and-white photo of Ricardo Flores Magón and his brother, Enrique. Both men had thick curly hair and identical handlebar mustaches. Ricardo's serious expres-sion and little round glasses gave him the aura of a philosopher.

The desert revolution was an international affair, inspired by the Magón brothers who ran the insurgency from their exile in General Otis's Los Angeles, just after the *LA Times* building was bombed by a pair of angry AFL labor activists, the McNamera brothers. That bombing led to a wave of anti-labor hysteria in Southern California, thus making the Magónista's assault on the sparsely populated border region improbable. The fact that both Otis and Spreckels had extensive land, water, and railroad hold-ings also assured that the odds were against them. Nonetheless, in January 1911 at the I.W.W. headquarters in Holtville, California, a group of mostly Mexican rebels loyal to Magón planned an at-tack on Mexicali. Soon afterwards, the rebel band captured Mexi-cali in a predawn raid, killing only the town jailor. Poor sap. The initial success of the raid led to a wave of support from famous voices on the left like Jack London and Emma Goldman, who spoke in San Diego to help rally workers to the cause. The rebels' biggest backers in the US were the Wobblies and Italian anar-chists, both of whose philosophies were in line with Magón's mix of Kropotkin, Bakunin, and Marx's. Simply put, Magón called upon the workers to "take immediate possession of the land, the machinery, the means of transportation and the buildings, with-out waiting for any law to decree it." Brutally treated by the Diaz dictatorship, and deeply committed to a utopian vision of communal society, Magón's idealism made him both admirable and seemingly unable to reconcile his dream with political reality. This last malady was something I had a soft spot for. Go figure.

Soon after the success at Mexicali, the rebels took Tecate, where they held off a lackluster attempt by the Mexican army to retake Mexicali. Despite this early success, factional squabbling broke out, and several leadership changes took place in the field. Many of the Mexicans who began the revolt left to fight with Madero, who was also challenging the Diaz regime. This resulted in the odd fact that a majority of the Magónista army was comprised of American Wobblies mixed with a few soldiers of fortune. With Magón permanently ensconced in Los Angeles, sending more anarchist pamphlets than bullets, the leadership ultimately fell to Caryl Rhys Pryce, a Welsh soldier of fortune who had fought in India and South Africa. A surreal pairing, I thought. Pryce fashioned himself a revolutionary and joined the Magónistas after reading a book on the murderous Diaz regime. His biggest victory came when he disobeyed orders from Magón, who wanted him to march east and fight the Mexican army, and instead turned westward to take Tijuana on May 9th, 1911. After a fierce fight, a rebel force of 220 men won a battle in which 32 people died. So the big victory had been an accident of sorts. You had to love it. I turned the page and glanced at a picture of Pryce standing with his hands on his hips, looking like a character in a TV Western. There was a crowd of men at his side, but their faces were indistinguishable. Could one have been Bobby Flash?

I looked at another picture of rebels standing in front of a line of storefronts where someone had replaced the Mexican flag with one reading, "*Tierra y Libertad*." It was after this victory that things turned bizarre, and dozens of sightseers from

San Diego, who had watched the battle from afar like a football game, flooded the town to loot the shops. With Magón still in Los Angeles, refusing to provide more aid to the untrustworthy Pryce, the rebels turned to revolutionary tourism and gambling to raise funds. It was a kind of Wobbly Vegas. Apparently, San Diegans were fascinated with the rugged revolutionary army, and would pay to take pictures with the wild mix of cowboys, Wobbly hobos, mercenaries, black army deserters, Mexicans, Indians, and random opportunists. I turned the page and stared at a photo of a group of Wobblies, Cocopah Indians, and African-American deserters, still in US uniforms, posing for a shot. No Bobby Flash.

It was during this period that Pryce met Daredevil Dick Ferris. I spotted a picture of Ferris, a pasty, pudgy specimen wearing a hat that made him look like a fading dandy. Today he'd be doing infomercials, I thought. Anyway, Ferris was a booster hired to drum up PR for San Diego and its upcoming Panama-California Exposition in Balboa Park. A shameless huckster, Ferris befriended Pryce, brought him to San Diego and sought to persuade him to support Ferris's notion of a "white man's republic" in lower Baja, Mexico. When Pryce proved to be of no use (he was arrested on his way back to Mexico and later abandoned the revolution altogether to act in Western movies), Ferris invented an imaginary invading army, going so far as to give a letter to the Mexican consul threatening an attack if Mexico refused to sell Lower Baja, and placing an ad in several newspapers looking for recruits. He even sent woman on horseback over the border to plant a flag in the name of "suffrage and model government." With these two stunts under his belt, he then recruited one of the remaining Magónista rebels to the Ferris cause and sent him back across the border to be nearly lynched by angry Wobblies who then elected Jack Mosby, one of their own, as the final commander of the doomed border revolution. I found a photo of Mosby, an unassuming man with a neatly trimmed mustache, wearing a battered fedora, and looking like a librarian with an ammo belt slung across his shoulder.

Led by Mosby, 150 Wobblies and 75 Mexicans took on 560 soldiers of the Mexican army on June 22nd, 1911. Badly outnumbered and low on supplies because of Magón's refusal to send more, the rebels were routed in three hours, with thirty killed, and the rest fleeing back across the border to be arrested by the United States army. Mosby was shot and killed when he tried to escape military custody. Ferris, shunned by Spreckels, went on the road to enact his version of the farce "The Man from Mexico" on stage. Magón died on the floor of a cell in Leavenworth after having been imprisoned for violating the Espionage Act during the first Red Scare. Bobby Flash? Somehow he made his way back to Holtville to end up on a Wanted poster with Gus Blanco. Then, under another name, he wound up running the gauntlet somewhere in San Diego in 1912. Nothing but traces of a remarkable life. I looked up, and the trolley was heading into San Ysidro. Time for my own trip across the border.

As I walked across the street toward the pedestrian bridge that takes you to the border I noticed the number of gringos headed over was much smaller than the last time I'd been to Tijuana. Almost everyone was Mexican—schoolchildren, maids, janitors, families returning from shopping trips. It seemed the drug wars in the city had scared away large numbers of Americans and forced a good number of Mexicans to do their business in San Diego. The economy probably wasn't helping either. I wove my way through the labyrinth of concrete, over the footbridge, past the Border Patrol cameras to the big metal turnstile that clanks loudly to announce every living soul leaving or coming home. On the other side, I saw Ricardo, and he met me with a smile and a firm handshake. I started in with my feeble present-tense Spanish, but it quickly became apparent that he spoke perfect English. When I told him that I'd been reading about Ricardo Flores Magón on the trolley, he responded, "No relation, but good choice" with a laugh. We walked by an empty police checkpoint to his car, an old Jeep, parked across the street from the outdoor sports book. I glanced over at a crowd of men drinking Tecates or coffee in styrofoam cups as they stared at the screens monitoring the horse races. We got in the Jeep and drove by a few abandoned curio shops and headed toward the working class section of the city, far from Avenida Revolución, the main tourist strip. The city seemed depressed and tense. I asked Ricardo about the lack of pedestrians coming south.

"*Revolución* is dead too, man," he said soberly. "Nothing happening there anymore, even on weekends. The drug wars and the economy in the north are killing the businesses." The papers had been full of news about murders and big shoot-outs even in broad daylight. Not even the hills where the middle class and the wealthy lived were safe anymore. A newspaper editor had been murdered and others had hired guards. Some police officials had been killed by the drug lords, others were on the take. Tourists had been robbed on the roads south to San Felipe and Ensenada. It was the Wild West. We cruised past a big open-air market full of stalls selling fruit, clothing, small electronic goods, and tacos. I caught a whiff of *carne asada* coming off a grill. It smelled good and I realized I was hungry. We turned down a street lined with small office fronts and pulled up in front of one with "*Justicia*" painted on the window.

Inside, I was greeted by a small, pretty woman named Gabriela, who would introduce me to the other women sitting in a circle of small metal chairs, chatting animatedly with each other.

The office was small with a big wooden desk that was littered with mail and notebooks. It had a phone but no computer. The women were sitting in a much larger meeting space, a large room with concrete walls and a concrete floor. It would have been ugly if not for the murals someone had painted all over the walls—there were portraits of Zapata, Ché Guevara, Subcommandante Marcos of the Zapatista front, and, interestingly, Ricardo Flores Magón, along with some beautiful nods to Mexican folk art including a *calavera* with fist upraised. I smiled, sat down on one of the metal chairs, and introduced myself. One of the women thanked me for coming and handed me a plate of *pan* she had made. I thanked her, took a piece, and listened to their stories.

None of the women spoke English so Ricardo and Gabriela served as translators as, one by one, the women told me about their lives. They lived in the neighborhood under an abandoned maquiladora as the letter Neville had passed on to me had said. Apparently the maquiladora up the hill was owned by a man who had closed down the shop without doing any cleanup, so the chemicals involved in making batteries were left under a big canvas tent. Once the tons of abandoned waste from the batteries began to seep into the earth, it entered the well that supplied the barrio down the hill. Worse still, when the rains came in the winter, the chemicals would get washed down the hill, through the dirt streets where their children played. One of the women, Marisol, a stout, kind-faced grandmother with lively eyes, had come with pictures of the waste heap, the neighborhood from above, and children playing soccer, kicking the ball through puddles of toxic waste. I surveyed the pictures and studied Marisol's face as she explained how it had begun with people getting sick to their stomachs or having their eyes burn for no apparent reason. Then there were strange cases of cancer, lots of them. And finally, mothers started giving birth to babies with terrible birth defects, babies with damaged brains or horrible disfigurements. By then, I was taking notes furiously, as one woman after another added her tale of betrayal.

I was particularly struck by the fact that these women still worked at other factories, for ten or twelve hours a day, and then came home to take care of their families. They woke before dawn, worked at home, at the factory, and at home again, and still found time to organize Las Madres Unidas against all odds. It was jaw-dropping. Another *madre*, Rosa, a sharp-eyed, middle-aged woman with obvious scars on her wiry arms and her fierce heart, angrily told me how the owner of the company had shut it down overnight, taken out the valuable equipment, and shipped it to China, where he had moved the operation because the labor was even cheaper there. NAFTA and Mexican law forbid such practices, but there were no enforcement clauses. The Mexican government ignored its own labor laws to appease the companies, and the United States ignored the matter altogether. All the while, the owner sat in a big house just across the border without a care in the world, fat and happy, as Rosa put it.

Finally, Isabel, a short, Indian-looking woman in her thirties, wearing a striking, hand-embroidered blouse and blue jeans told me about how the closing of the plant had changed the life of the barrio. Most of the people in the neighborhood had moved there to work for the factory on the hill. They came, built their own houses out of what they could—with no infrastructure, no water, no help from the government or the company. When the company left, they all had to get jobs elsewhere, further away, so the walk took an hour each way. The women had no protection on their walks and some had disappeared like the women in Juarez. They could not trust the police, and the other factory owners would not provide transportation and punished them if they arrived late or left early. It was a house of pain, I thought to myself as I looked into the faces of these women, faces lined with worry, work, and suffering. Still there was fight in them—hope against all odds. I promised them that I would tell their tale and come back to see their neighborhood with a photographer. Then I thanked them for their stories and shook each of their hands like a prayer for more power than I had to redress their great wrongs.

It was dark outside as Ricardo drove me back to the border. He thanked me for coming and I told him it was my pleasure to do what I could to tell this story. We made plans for my return visit to tour the neighborhood. The lights in the hills twinkled a reddish-yellow and car horns blared angrily in the rush hour traffic. He let me off at the end of a long line to get back. "Goodbye, my friend," he said before driving off into the night. I dropped a coin in a basket at the feet of an ancient Indian woman, who was begging on a dirty wool blanket by the line. Some little girls sold me a pack of gum and I looked over at a line of shops hawking cheap liquor and pharmaceuticals for those returning to the land of the free. In line, I closed my eyes and listened to the distant strains of music from the Mexican street blending with hundreds of car radios talking in Spanish and English. AC/DC and Los Tigres del Norte. At the end of the line, the guards regarded me suspiciously as they always seemed to do. They sternly pulled aside the whole family behind me and took them to secondary inspection as I headed to the trolley. On the way back, the train was half empty and I closed my eyes and tried to fall asleep with visions of Las Madres Unidas dancing in my head.

3

The next morning I hit the *New Sun* office early again and started on a piece about Las Madres. It came easily. The women's faces and stories were fresh in my mind, and I wrote with a sharp-edged anger. I had called the company office and got a generic corporate denial of any knowledge of the situation. Las Madres had found the home address and phone number of the owner, so I called his house and didn't get any further than "How did you get this number?" They sounded worried and that made me happy. When Neville came in, I showed him what I had started and he loved it.

"We'll make it a cover piece once you get some pictures," he said. I called up the freelancer and got on her calendar. The neighborhood tour wasn't for another two weeks, however, so I had some time to kill. I noticed that the answering machine was blinking and I checked and found a message from the Marine. He could meet me tomorrow. I called to confirm and then left for the day to go to the Historical Society.

Even during the worst bust since the Great Depression, San Diego looked like Disneyland compared to Tijuana. Everything was newer and brighter—at least it seemed that way. I had taken my car to work today so I drove across the Laurel Street bridge off 6th into Balboa Park with the California Tower rising like Xanadu in the bright January sky. It was one of those summer-in-winter days, and the park was a gorgeous apparition in all its Spanish revival glory. I remembered reading that some of the Wobblies who'd fled the second battle of Tijuana ended up working on the construction projects for the Panama California Exposition. It was ironic that they'd escaped from a failed border revolution to help construct an Anglo fantasy of California's Spanish golden era. It was Spreckels's fear that the Wobblies would piss on San Diego's party in 1915 that led to the brutal response to the free speech fighters as early as 1911. Irony heaped upon irony. I smiled at the still-beautiful flowers and fountains and Spreckels Organ Pavilion as I drove to the small lot by the archery range to park.

Down in the basement of the Historical Society, I looked through everything I could find: postcards of dead Wobblies on the battlefield after Mosby's forces were routed, photos of the crowds being hit by firehouses, a picture of Wobblies posing on a hijacked train in Mexico, a shot of a Wobbly holding up a copy of *Industrial Worker* with a story about the fight in San Diego, and several portraits of soapboxers speaking to crowds at Heller's Corner, their arms outstretched, their fists clenched, a sea of men in battered hats below them—tired, scarred, bruised, but defiant faces. I was almost through with the binder when I came upon a striking image of a rough-looking character sitting on the steps outside the I.W.W. headquarters. He had a full beard and a big, flat, boxer's nose. His upper lip hung over his lower lip. He was staring hard into the camera, with a "get that thing away from me" look. He had on overalls and a black felt hat. On the back of the picture someone had written, "I.W.W. Agitator" and, after that, a different hand had written "Bunco." I asked the woman behind the counter if she knew anything about the change. She didn't. I dug out my photocopy of the Wanted poster and reread the description of Gus Blanco or "Bunco." It certainly could have been him with his beard grown out.

After I was done with the photographs I looked through some old copies of the *Labor Leader* for news on Bobby or Blanco and struck out. The vertical files had some of the same articles I found at the library, but nothing that referred to individual Wobblies.

Leaving the vertical files, I asked for the court records for 1912 and found a record of the arrest of "Buckshot Jack," but no references to a trial or even a mugshot. Perhaps "Buckshot" never went to trial because he was taken up to run the gauntlet instead. If they had only known, he would have been shipped back to Holtville. Nothing on Blanco.

Finally, I came across the personal papers of a labor leader who had been in the local Communist Party in the 1930s. There were lots of things, letters mostly, about the battles for control of the San Diego Labor Council, but nothing about the I.W.W. until I found some much later letters to his daughter about being interviewed by a college student about the free speech fight:

> I spoke a while last week with a young fellow studying the history of the free speech fights in the teens. He seemed very earnest and disappointed that I had been too young to have been involved in the organizing. I did tell him a few stories about sneaking out to watch the commotion on the streets and remembering the fire hoses and the horrible police swinging away at the crowds. There were stories about people being kidnapped and never being seen again. It seems like another lifetime now. The fellow's name was Sam Jones.

The letter moved on to other matters. Not much to work with, but I did write down Jones's name. Maybe he had done a thesis or something. All in all it was a disappointing day. The archivist recommended I try the court records out in the Imperial Valley and then wrote down the titles of a handful of dissertations and Master's theses on the free speech fight. He also told me to try the Library for Progressive Research in Los Angeles, and Wayne State University's archives in Detroit. With no new leads and a stack of homework, I left for the day, not sure if my big idea would work out. Perhaps Bobby Flash was lost to history. Hell, I didn't even know much about my own family's distant past, no less the history of strangers. Still, I was haunted by the image of Bobby's face, like my son's face, receding into the past and merging in my mind's eye.

Out on the Prado I walked by the reflecting pool, stopped to watch the gigantic koi swimming around lazily, and took a stroll through the botanical garden before heading over to the café by the art museum for a cup of coffee. As I sat down, I remembered that I should write Hank back before too long, so I tore a piece of paper out of my notebook and did my best job of playing a father. I encouraged Hank to stay in school while acknowledging his point about how uninspiring the classes could be. I joked, self-effacingly and with sufficient irony, about him not following my example in terms of career. I tried to assure him that what seemed like an endless time at home was really not that long. How was his mother, really? Etc. Despite having been at it for over twenty years now, some part of me still felt as if I was putting on an act as a father. Don't get me wrong, I loved Hank fiercely, but who was I to tell anybody anything about anything? It was funny, in my role as a reporter, I could hammer away at people with no hesitation and no regrets, but as a father I felt unqualified to give the simplest advice. I was utterly humbled by the nakedness of Hank's need for my love and the possibility that withholding it, even unconsciously, could burden him forever.

I remember when, as a young boy, Hank would ask me an endless series of questions, from the mundane to the profound. It was everything from "Why do elephants have long noses?" and "Why are clouds big and small?" to "What is God?" and "Why do people die?" Sometimes I'd come up with crazy answers to make him laugh, but I knew when I was serious that Hank trusted me totally and that I couldn't let him down. So while we had great fun with some of his queries, I'd sometimes be hit by a terror that my answers would harm him somehow. When he asked, "Why does grandma say bad things?" I knew those things were about me, and I fought a gut-wrenching mixture of rage and shame and helplessness, as I looked into his earnest little face, his big eyes watching my every move.

Other than our too-infrequent visits, I knew my son through letters, first in crayon, then pencil, then pen, then word-processed. I had them all in binders: colorful, primitive sketches of baseball players, guys playing guitar, animals at the zoo all with captions and short stories like "The Hippos eat lunch at the zoo and miss their families in Africa" or "Rock stars make people dance and sing." Then, later on, I would get confessions about crushes or philosophical musings about something he'd read. That was one thing I'd credit Trish with, she always had him reading. In one letter he told me he'd read "Sonny's Blues" by James Baldwin, back when he was in high school, and said he thought he understood what the jazz player meant by "the storm inside":

> The brothers are talking about suffering but I think it's more than just Sonny's heroin addiction. It's about the fact that everybody suffers and there isn't any way to escape it. The only thing that people can do is use their pain to create something beautiful—otherwise it will eat them up or kill them. That's why Sonny's brother finally comes to see him as royalty. His music is how he lives and connects with the world. Maybe it's that way with your writing? I don't know yet what my thing is. Maybe I never will. Who knows? Anyway, it was a good story. Better than what I read in class.

Stuff like that always floored me. He was a remarkable kid, but how the hell could I respond to that? My son, musing on the meaning of suffering in his middle teens. Was I the source? I would always write back and treat him seriously, but I never knew if I was doing any good.

Perhaps I was so unsure of myself as a father because I didn't really have one myself. My own father died of a heroin overdose in 1975 when I was just a kid. Mom, or Sandy as I more often called her, left him, with me in tow, sometime in the early seventies. So I only remember my father vaguely in flashes of memory—running with me on the beach with his long hair and shaggy beard, playing guitar for me in the basement of a large Victorian house in San Francisco, carrying me on his bare shoulders on a hike in Topanga Canyon. I had a picture of him that I kept in the drawer next to my bed while I was growing up. It was a shot of him standing beside a big psychedelic school bus wearing a plain gray t-shirt, smiling a beatific smile. On the back, my grandmother (on my dad's side) had written, "Your Dad."

The story I grew up with was that Joe—that was his name—had gotten hooked on drugs and "abandoned the family." He was a bum, a bad man, just like his granddad "the radical" had been. Both my mother and her family spouted that line as did Chad, my stepdad from the time I was thirteen or so. Since my grandfather had died in World War II they spared his memory. I never heard any version of Dad's death from his family since Sandy had cut off all contact with them when she left him. Later, in my teens, I was told that he had died in the back of a bus while he was following the Grateful Dead on their 1975 tour. When I looked up the Dead's tour history in a book at the library and found out that the band had been on hiatus that year, Sandy had to confess that she didn't know or care when or where he died, that she had simply gotten a note from Joe's mother informing her that he had overdosed. She hadn't gone to the funeral or even bothered to tell me for a couple of years. It was then, during that confrontation, that I learned that Sandy had left him, not the other way around. He was still a bum though, that was not in question. Even my great grandfather, whom she had never met, was a bad seed. Somehow Joe and his grandfather's brief, shadowy reunion was to blame for my father's drug addiction. Some shit like that. It was all stacked against me. What were my chances?

So I grew up with a gaping hole in my family history that Sandy thought she'd plastered over when she married Chad. When we moved into his house, Chad had only met me briefly, a handful of times, before leaving on dates with Sandy, but still he proclaimed, "Well, looks like I'm your Dad now, Jackie." I told him that he wasn't and he told me not to "disrespect him," and we were off to a flying start. Chad's strategy was to make a point of how my real dad was a "hippie loser" and that he had stepped up "like a man and a provider" to save the day. He was a world-class asshole. I hated his guts at hello in the way that only a thirteen-year-old boy can hate—full of passionate intensity.

As I got older, I made a point of finding ways to irritate Chad and expose his hypocrisy. The day after he gave me a "just say no" lecture, I stole his pot and smoked it in my room. When he talked about developing a work ethic, I skipped school and got drunk. After he stuck a "Ronald Reagan for President" sticker on our car, I peeled it off. You see, Chad was one of those self-indulgent baby boomers who did the sixties and disco thing and then, seamlessly, in the eighties, got amnesia to go along with their greed and vanity. His Achilles' heel was that he still liked to party with the boys from the ad agency and this hypocrisy made him a ripe target for an angry teenage boy looking for trouble. When I stole his vial of cocaine and lined the coke up to spell "Chad" on the living room coffee table, he hit the ceiling. I could hear him screaming at Sandy, who was at her wit's end, for hours about what a worthless piece of shit I was, etc. Finally, they came up with the solution of sending me to Catholic school to get me some discipline and a good value system. "You mean you don't want me to go to school with black kids, right?" I snarled. Chad slapped me, and told me that I could leave now and he wouldn't mind. That led to another brawl with Sandy, but I ultimately submitted to going to Our Lady of the Sorrows after she begged me, with tears and all, to do it for her.

Our Lady of the Sorrows wasn't nearly as bad as I had imagined. Growing up, we'd never spent a second in church so the whole thing was pretty amusing to me. It turned out that I liked the short skirts that the girls had to wear. I liked talking to Father Hatch about philosophy after Religious Studies class. I even enjoyed doing bong loads with Brother O'Hara after Literature class. Lit was in the final period, and we'd meet at his apartment a mile or so from campus (not all of the brothers lived in the rectory). He was gay and looking for a little I'm sure, but I was pretty wise to it and he had really good weed. "Dude, I'm no Altar Boy," I said one time after an awkward hand on the shoulder moment. After that, we were cool. It was bong loads, rapping about *Zen and the Art of Motorcycle Maintenance* or some other book, and no funny business.

Hatch, on the other hand, was straight and had a bit of a roving eye at that. He was a Jesuit who had a Ph.D. in philosophy and used to loan me books on existentialism and say, "It's my job to tell you not to take this too seriously." We'd look at girls sometimes and he'd asked me who I thought was the prettiest so he could enter the conversation through the side door and say something like, "I see your point, Wilson." The rest of the priests and brothers were pretty hardcore alcoholics. Sometimes a brother would get shipped off to rehab and they'd tell us that "Brother So-and-So had been reassigned by the Diocese." That happened to Father McNulty after he made the local news for drowning the stray cats that'd been keeping him up all night by howling outside the rectory. A local trouble-shooter made him "turkey of the week." Stuff like that went on all the time. It blew my mind at first, but I got used to it.

It wasn't just the priests and brothers who were a little off center, either. The president of the school got busted for tax evasion while I was there, and another teacher got caught in a drug scandal when the police found her buying coke from Jared Stone in the back of his bitchin' black Camaro. To me, the oddest thing was "Father Chardonnay Week" when they'd have us write letters to the Pope to ask him to canonize Chardonnay, the founder of the order of brothers who ran the school (Hatch and O'Hara were free agents of a sort). Apparently, Chardonnay had refused to pay taxes to the French after the government demanded them following the Revolution. He was kind of the Howard Jarvis of aspiring saints I guess, a perfect spiritual exemplar for the Reagan Revolution. I used to get detention for writing letters to the Pope that started with lines like "Hey Big" or "Your Super Holiness." An exercise like that was just hard to take seriously.

What I liked best was football. If I had gone to a bigger, public school, I would have never been able to make a team. But with only about 500 students in all, Our Lady of the Sorrows had to take all comers. I was small, fast, and fearless, but my hands were useless. Hence, I wound up on coverage as a gunner. I'd jet down the field and hurl myself recklessly at the return man. I loved the contact, the pure violence of the hit. And the coach loved me. He called me "Smackin'" Jack Wilson. It was stupid, but amusing. Coach would make me take it easy in practice, but in games, he'd slap me on the helmet and say, "Knock 'em dead kid." He left the God stuff in church, too. I liked that. We were simply there to play football. Not that we won many games, but I appreciated the honesty of his approach. And on Friday nights, I'd dole out vicious hits, balling up all of my unfocused rage and hurling it at some poor kid from St. Mary's or Blessed Heart.

My best friend on the team—and in school, for that matter—was Shane Black. Shane was bigger than me and could catch, so he played tight end, and even started. He got me into punk rock and helped me get a fake ID. We shaved our heads, which allowed us to move easily between the vastly different worlds of Catholic school, football, and punk clubs. I loved the pit; when the crowd was at its most frenzied, I'd be at the heart of it, slam dancing, jumping on and off the stage. I felt at home in the community of alienated kids I met at shows. It was a beloved community of sorts. Still, at some of the shows it would get nasty, particularly at the Olympic, downtown. I remember coming home with a split lip from the slam pit at a Black Flag show and telling Sandy I did it in football practice. Chad was puzzled by this phenomenon. He couldn't understand what wasn't cool about Foghat, Foreigner, and Bad Company. "Why don't you listen to normal music?" he'd whine. "Is this what they're teaching you at Our Lady of the Sorrows?" He tried to send me to a psychologist, but Sandy got me out of that by noting that my grades were still good.

It was at a Dead Kennedy's show at a roller rink in the East Valley that I met my first long-term girlfriend, Beth Stein. I ran back from the pit when some idiot started pulling the tube lights down from the ceiling and raining shattered glass on the crowd. I got a bad cut on my head and Beth came over with a handkerchief and helped me stop the bleeding. Afterward, we made out in the parking lot and had sex in the back of her Volkswagen Bug. She had big, warm brown eyes and full lips. Her hair was blue and she was wearing an oversized, white DKs t-shirt, a long black skirt, and Doc Martens. She had a nose ring. Her parents lived in a large ranch house in Tarzana in the West Valley, not far from Chad's place in Northridge. They disapproved of me because I wasn't Jewish, and they refused to speak to me when I came over to pick her up. It was like being invisible. Her mother was waiting for her to get over this strange phase and marry a doctor, so she'd set up dates for her with men in their early thirties. Beth would tell her mother she was going to meet them and drive over to my house. It was a weird scene, but I liked her a lot. We'd talk about music mostly and books we'd read. Joy Division and *Steppenwolf* by Herman Hesse. Beth was on the pill so we had lots of sex too. She was a fantastic girl, full of life and keen intelligence. I was enthralled.

So life went on merrily for me and, in my senior year, I actually got accepted to UCLA, as did Shane. Unfortunately, Chad and Sandy were fighting all the time and, just as I was getting ready to graduate, Chad started humping some bimbo in Santa Monica and Sandy was going crazy. She'd drive over the hill and sit in her car outside the bimbo's apartment. Chad, heartless bastard that he was, would come over to the window and wave to her before he drew the drapes closed and got busy. He moved out in my last month of high school and, during one of their last arguments, he made it clear that I wasn't going to UCLA. "That little shit can get a job and pay his own way," was how he put it. Soon afterwards, Chad sold the house in Northridge and kept the money. Sandy's friends told her to sue him for alimony and get the house, but Sandy wouldn't do it. "I don't need anything from him," she'd say. I couldn't blame her, though her nobility cost me a shot at going to a four-year school. About the same time, Beth told me she was going to NYU. I couldn't blame her either.

Sandy moved into a two-bedroom apartment in the East Valley and I stuck with her for a while. I forgave her for her bad choices and shoddy mothering and she forgave me for being a total shit. We bonded in our regret. I even grew my hair out to make her happy and started calling her Mom once in a while. The thing I came to understand was that she had married Chad because she really believed I needed a father. Sure, it was a train wreck, but it was a well-intentioned one. Sandy kept her job as a secretary in some generic office park in Thousand Oaks and we shared the rent. I had to pick up the costs for the classes I was taking at Valley College, which meant working at whatever I could get. It was in the middle of the Reagan recession so I did a little bit of everything—mostly shitwork.

My first job was as a stock boy at Auto World, a cavernous warehouse where retailers and auto shops came to buy parts wholesale. I spent eight hours a day unloading trucks of auto parts. The trucks would come in, one after the other, and I'd meet them on a forklift at the loading dock. At 8:00 AM, it was a single truck full of brake shoes. Two trailer loads of mufflers at 10:00 AM, a truck of radiator hoses after lunch. Then it would be more mufflers in the early afternoon and a semi full of rims at 4:00 PM. The culture of the warehouse was hard and profane. Everyone had an unwanted nickname. My name was "College Boy" because I had stupidly mentioned my pathetic attempt at education on the side. This led to my getting tossed into the worst jobs, if at all possible.

"I bet College Boy has never unloaded a crate of mufflers in a hundred degree heat before," Big Frank would say sarcastically before sending me out on the forklift at the peak of the midday inferno to meet the truck and then sort the mufflers after they had been sitting in the sun getting hot enough to burn my hands through gloves. I did it and didn't grouse about it. This gained me some grudging respect. Frank called everyone else by an ethnic slur or a demeaning insult. So "the kike" and "the spic" worked alongside "Lard Ass Larry" and "Shit for Brains," as Frank lovingly referred to them. If you bitched, it only got piled on thicker. When the fat trucker who always ate our last few donuts got to the box before Frank could grab his jellyroll, he made sure to load up the next day's batch with a box full of Ex-Lax, so fatso had to call in sick and get his pay docked. When the delivery guy from UPS cussed us out for making him wait, Frank made sure he had to wait five minutes longer each subsequent day that week. "Fuckwad" was the driver's name from then on out.

After work, we'd grab a twelve-pack and sit on the loading dock, staring at the teenage girls at the bus stop across the street. I began to see that the dirty jokes and the tall tales the guys told masked a longing and a sense of dread that the joys of their high school days might have been their lives' high-water mark. Frank, the floor boss, was older and made more money, but his coarseness covered over the fact that he'd never be a "college boy" like the suit in the front office who worked in air conditioning and got to order Frank around. One day, after Frank had been particularly tough on me, I was hanging mufflers on the top tier of the catwalk in the airplane-hanger-sized warehouse, when he came up to me and pulled a vial of coke out of his pocket and offered me a snort. I took it and he said, "Now work faster, you little asshole." It's strange to say, but the gesture was almost tender, which I found a little moving. Unfortunately for everyone, Frank's generosity with the crew was caught on the surveillance cameras the suit had installed over the weekend, and we were all on the street within a week.

My stint at Auto World was followed by a job in an insurance records warehouse in Pacoima. There, my job was to unload boxes from a huge truck that came every morning at nine. Once I had my mountain of boxes, the truck left and, for the rest of the day, I was supposed to shelve the boxes in numerical order until there were no more boxes. My "supervisor" was a cool Chicano guy in his early thirties named Cheno. Cheno sat at a desk by the door, read the newspaper, and listened to the radio. If it wasn't for the music, we would both have gone crazy. We listened to rock stations, the news, even "Literature Hour" on public radio. I could easily do the entire load in half a day, so I would lag, stop and sit on the boxes, or walk over to rap with Cheno about whatever was on his mind at the moment. Cheno was a philosopher of sorts so he would frequently have some big thought on his mind like, "If everyone decided there was no God, would people be better or worse?" Cheno's take was that they would be worse. "It would be the war of all against all man. People are low, you know what I mean?"

"I don't know, man. Religion has actually *started* more wars than it's stopped," I replied.

"Don't get me wrong," Cheno said, "I don't believe in anything, man. I just think people need something to keep them in line so they don't go *totally loco*." I laughed, grabbed a Coke from the dirty little fridge by his desk and walked outside for some air. Right next to the records warehouse was a porn warehouse. They threw away damaged product in a big dumpster that they kept locked up like Fort Knox. Once in a while, a page would come loose and we'd find a random beaver shot lying on the ground. Cheno collected these and had lined the wall above his desk with them, creating a perverse collage.

Next to the porn mill was another building that was always sealed up tight. I could hear the drone of loud machinery, but I never saw a soul, until that day when I was standing by the porn dumpster with my Coke and somebody rolled up the big metal door to reveal rows of sewing machines, each one the host to a woman, hunched over with head down, hands and fingers moving fast and furious over a garment. They all looked Indian. It was a hot summer day in the nineties and I was surprised to see that the huge sweatshop was only cooled by a single large fan. The women, both young and old, looked exhausted, with faces like marathon runners nearing the finish line. It was only two o'clock. The man who'd rolled up the door glared at me and said, "Mind your own business if you know what's good for you." He pulled the door down and it slammed against the concrete like a prison cell.

When I went back inside to tell Cheno, he shook his head and said, "They're slaves, Jack."

"What?" I said incredulously.

"Serious, man, they don't have no papers. They come up to get work and those fuckers grab them and tell them they have to work fourteen hours a day, and if they quit or tell the cops they'll be deported away from their children. What do you call that but slavery, man?"

"Shit," I said, unable to muster anything more profound.

"No kidding, Jack," Cheno said. "No kidding."

Early the next morning a man from the main office came, took a walk around with a clipboard, and left without speaking to us. Pilar, who drove the morning truck, told us she had heard they were getting ready to close us down. Then she slipped me her phone number. That night, we went out for beers, Pilar and me. We met at a little dive in Sylmar and played pool. She had big brown eyes and a sexy, crooked smile. She always wore her hair in pigtails under her hat at work. Without the hat and uniform, she was striking in a plain white blouse and tight jeans. She took me home and we made love all night. She had beautiful, long black hair, which she took down for the first time before we got into bed. It transformed her miraculously from a tomboy to a goddess. When I left in the rosy dawn I asked when I could see her again. "Never," she said as she kissed me goodbye and patted my cheek. "My boyfriend would kill you."

I missed Pilar and Cheno, but losing that job allowed me to focus a bit more on the last two weeks of my summer courses in English and Journalism. It turned out that, according to my professors, I was a good writer. Still, at this rate, I wondered if I'd ever be able to finish before I hit thirty. I got two A's and signed up for another journalism class that Fall. In the meantime, I went to a temp agency and they found me a job at an office for once. It was mind numbing. My task was to cross-check thousands of names, addresses, and phone numbers on the company computer with the same names, addresses, and phone numbers in an endless series of big plastic binders. This was supposed to last for two weeks. I got fired in half a day when the supervisor caught me putting my feet up on the desk during a break. "It sends the wrong message," he said. I told him to go fuck himself, and he called for security to have me escorted from of the building. As soon as we were out of earshot, the guard said, "Good job in there, kid." I laughed and we shook hands before parting ways.

The temp agency told me on the phone that I wasn't the caliber of employee they were accustomed to working with. I hung up on the woman and found a job in the want ads at The Royal Ribbon Company, a computer printer ribbon factory over the hill downtown. My shift started at 5:00 AM, so the drive from the valley was relatively painless. The job, on the other hand, was grueling. I started at a station that received a constant flow of boxes of newly inked ribbons (these were the days of big old printers) and I had to unload the box, ribbon by ribbon, and wipe off the excess ink with a rag that I dipped in a toxic-smelling cleaning solution. I wore big rubber gloves, but, by the end of the day, my hands were still dyed black and blue from the ink. It took me half an hour of scrubbing every day to get clean. Homero, the fellow next to me at this station, had worked there for five years and his hands stayed dyed, even after he scrubbed down. That can't be healthy, I thought, but I needed the money.

If the ink-stained hands weren't bad enough, the lifting did the trick. The boxes were all around fifty pounds, easy enough to lift and stack, but by the end of the day, my back was sore as hell. But I stuck with it, working like a robot on the line. Homero was a stoic, nearly silent man who only grunted when I tried to speak with him—in English at first, and later in Spanish. I was the only Anglo in the whole factory it turned out. Everyone else was Mexican, or from Guatemala, Nicaragua, El Salvador, or some other country in Central America. There was a crew of workers from Pakistan too. And one black guy, George, whom I had lunch with every day.

"What brings you to the neighborhood, white boy?" was the first thing out of his mouth. He grinned and laughed at me before I had a chance to answer.

"I'm on a field trip," I said. George had just got out of high school and was trying to save enough money to move back to Alabama where his extended family lived. His parents had worked at the shipyards in Long Beach and at an auto factory in Southeast LA, but those jobs were drying up or long gone. And his neighborhood was getting pretty rough too.

"All these illegals are fucking things up," he said.

"Don't you think it's bigger than them?" I responded, remembering the sweatshop in Pacoima.

"Maybe," he said, "But when you only got a small pie, you don't invite the neighbors over for dessert." I laughed and let the matter rest. We were sitting on the loading dock, watching our fellow workers as they huddled by their cars listening to a soccer match on their radios. It was the Cupa de los Americas, and Mexico was playing Guatemala. Mexico scored and a wave of cheers went up just as the horn sounded signifying the end of our leisure. Back inside, the noise was deafening. I looked over at the station where the boss had put the group from Pakistan. A big guy saw me and gave me a hostile stare. I ignored him and put on my rubber gloves. Across the floor I could see the prettiest woman in the factory, Rosa, whispering to another woman, who then whispered something to another woman. She saw me looking over and smiled at me. I smiled back and started going about my work.

At the end of our shift she walked over to me and said, "The girls think your blue eyes are pretty."

"And you?" I asked, surprised and intrigued.

"I don't trust them," she said smiling as she walked away. That night I got a call from Shane who was at UCLA. He had a friend who worked at a local weekly called *Word on the Street*. They were looking for student interns. It didn't pay, but it would give me some experience. I took down the information and told Shane I'd call the next day after work.

At Royal Ribbon, the flirtation stopped but the whispering continued. At the break, George and I watched Rosa walk over to the big Pakistani who had glared at me. Their talk didn't last long and Rosa left looking frustrated.

"What's going on?" I asked George.

"She trying to organize, Jack."

"Organize what?" I asked stupidly.

"A union, white boy. She talked to me the other day and I told her I don't need the trouble."

"She told me she didn't trust my eyes," I said with a smirk.

"She don't trust you because she don't think you're gonna stay long. Are you?"

"No," I acknowledged. "No fucking way." The rest of the day dragged on horribly. My eyes had started to dry out from the fumes and my back was mighty sore. I felt bad that Rosa didn't trust me enough to let me in on the secret. Did she think I was a spy or something? That was a little paranoid, I thought. Was it because I was white? Depressing. That afternoon, I called the *Word on the Street* and they asked me to come in for an interview. I was excited at the possibility of learning how to write for a paper. I'd been driving forklifts and lifting boxes for over a year and it was getting old.

Back at Royal Ribbon, I kept my head down for a few more weeks until, one day, the boss came over, pulled Rosa off the line, and took her into his office. She came out in tears with a security guard at each arm, escorting her out of the building. Then, I was surprised to see a whole bunch of other guards show up and take up positions at practically every station in the factory. Suddenly, the line stopped, and a phalanx of managers came out of the front office, splitting into pairs to hit each station. They were carrying batches of checks. When two of the little toads made their way over to Homero and me, we were told that, unfortunately, the factory was going to cease production. He handed me a check. I suddenly felt stupid and ashamed. Rosa had been right to be cautious of a stranger. They were firing the whole fucking plant, shutting it down to kill Rosa's organizing drive in utero. Most of the workers had no papers, so what could they do? It was unbelievable. The next day I checked the *Times* on a hunch and there it was: "Wanted, factory workers. Will Train. Contact Royal Ribbon Company."

I got the internship with *Word on the Street*, so I started doing a little bit of everything for them—reviews, reporting, editing. It was great. To pay the bills, I got a job at a home repair company, that consisted of Dan, the owner, and whoever happened to be working with him that week. We painted houses on the cheap, put in tile floors, replaced windows, etc. Dan was a great old guy, about sixty with a scruffy gray beard that made him look like a disheveled Hemingway with a beer gut. He could fix anything. His mornings were always productive and we'd be on pace to get done early, but then he'd grab a sixer at lunch and things slowed down considerably. He listened to AM radio news all day and would say things like, "The world's going to hell, drink up." His wife had died a few years before and his son was in the army, stationed in Germany. Once he had gotten a little drunk, he'd always put down his paintbrush or saw or spackle knife, slap me on the back and say, "You're a good worker, kid. Your Dad should be proud of you." He was a sweet, lonely old man so I never had the heart to tell him the truth.

4

I met the Marine, Mark Sawyer, at a Mexican restaurant in a strip mall next to an auto parts store in Oceanside. We sat down over enchiladas and talked about his buddy, Jake Sullivan. Mark was polite and very articulate, but you could see the weight he carried in his eyes. His clean-cut appearance and studied dignity covered over a deeper hurt. I got the sense that he was holding onto a certain formality as a way of overcoming his knowledge that chaos was somewhere just around the corner. He told me about his two tours in Iraq with Sullivan, a decorated war hero who became infuriated about human rights abuses by private contractors in Al Anbar province and complained to the higher ups only to be warned to mind his own business. Sadly, it was a familiar story by now. What bothered Mark, however, was his belief that everyone had turned the page on Iraq, even before it was over. As he put it, "It's as if our series got cancelled because of bad ratings. Everyone just changed the channel."

But for Jake, it wasn't that easy. He kept at it and got the information to some journalists who covered the story and it caused a stir. Jake got transferred to another unit and, when he came home after his second tour, his father, a career Marine, let him know he did not approve of his whistle blowing. That led Jake into a long depression that was exacerbated by his emerging posttraumatic stress, which the VA took its time to diagnose and treat. Jake went down hill, drank too much, and got into trouble—bar fights and a couple of DUI arrests. His girlfriend left him, and then he got a letter telling him that he was being called back up due to a shortage of manpower.

About that time, Mark told me, he and Jake went on a long

camping trip out in the desert. They spent a week hiking brutal, obscure trails in the mountains around Anza Borrego, and exploring the badlands. Things had been going fairly well until the night that Jake wanted to do the mushrooms he'd scored from some hippies on the boardwalk in Ocean Beach and Mark refused, sticking instead with a bottle of whiskey and The Doors on a boom box by the campfire. Jake got mad, told him to fuck off, and ate them anyway, wandering off by himself into the night without a flashlight or anything else. Mark let him go, waited for hours, but then started getting worried. It was probably three o'clock in the morning and he could hear a pack of coyotes howling in the near distance. Mark started searching the ravines near their camp, and he came up empty, but continued for hours into the dawn.

Mark kept looking for Jake, systematically mapping the land, quadrant by quadrant. Finally, he found Jake's clothes in a pile by some large rocks. He climbed up a steep hill in the morning light for what must have been several miles, then suddenly, from out of nowhere, he heard the sound of weeping above him and scurried faster until he came upon a small cave under several large boulders. It was then that the weeping turned to a moan and then a howl from what seemed like the bowels of the earth itself. Mark screamed out Jake's name and got no answer, so he climbed down into the cave, following the sound, until he found Jake lying on his back in the dark, his face and upper torso scratched bloody by his own hands.

He cradled Jake there for a long time saying only "It's alright" over and over in the calmest voice he could muster. Finally, Jake said "I'm sorry" and that was the first and last that they ever spoke about it. Mark led him out of the cave, back down to his clothing, and they returned to camp, cleaned up as best they could, and drove home in silence.

In the days that followed, Jake retold the story of their trip to several mutual friends editing out the nightmare hike. Mark thought he should have told Jake to get some help, but he seemed more normal for a while. When the subject of returning to Iraq came up, Jake began to welcome it; he said he wanted to go back. It would get him straight. Then, without a word, the day before he was supposed to leave, he shot himself. And nobody covered it.

Mark's lips tightened as he told the story. "How can a Purple Heart make the news, but not his death?" I shook my head and told him I'd do my best to tell the story, tie it in to the unexpected rise in suicides amongst service men. He shook my hand and thanked me, quite formally, and we walked out to the parking lot together and parted ways.

As I hit the 5 south and drove back to the office, I thought back to my early days in San Diego when I used to hang out in the old downtown with all the dives full of jarheads and sailors playing pool. At first, I have to admit, I had some politically correct, punk disdain for them, but, after a few conversations, I dropped my attitude and got to know some of them. They were kids mostly, looking for adventure or a way to pay for college or stay out of jail. I even had some great conversations with guys who were reading Noam Chomsky or some other radical stuff, while they did their time in the belly of the beast. It complicated things for me. Not that I'm any less anti-war, I just put the blame where it belongs: at the top. Actually meeting guys in the service moved my opposition to war from an abstraction to a visceral anger at the waste of life.

I had come down to San Diego to write for the *SD Scene*, an offshoot of the *LA Scene,* in the early nineties. After Trisha left, I'd stayed in Los Angeles for a while but it felt purgatorial, even when I moved back to Venice to escape the Valley. A change of venue was in order. The owners of the *LA Scene* had sent my friend and fellow reporter, Gary, down to San Diego in the late eighties to start up a new paper. I'd gone down to visit Gary a number of times before I transferred to San Diego, and we'd spent a few lost weekends hitting the handful of rock clubs in the Gaslamp and following them up with a delirious trail of dives: the Hong Kong, the Naha, the Orient, Suzy Wong's, the Li Po, Molly's, the Lobby, etc. If the bars closed too early, we'd hitch a ride to TJ and drink in the Zona Norte until they shut down at 6:00 AM, staggering into the early dawn to buy cheap cigarettes and tacos on the street before figuring out how to get home. I remember waking up on Gary's couch with a surreal thread of memories of pool tables next to fish tanks; odd conversations with aging Korean barmaids who longed for the old days; sailors fighting with fists and pool sticks; Patsy Cline and Asian disco on the jukebox; tequila shots in Mexican dance halls filled with campesinos, tough prostitutes, and taxi cab dealers; bodies sleeping on the benches in the billiards hall; Norteño and filterless Delicato cigarettes; storefront evangelical churches preaching all night; and the rush and bustle of the 4:00 AM street on Friday.

I came to love all the old dives downtown and got to know some of the bartenders and doormen. The old timers had years of stories to tell and the gritty Gaslamp would have made Bukowski proud, with its bittersweet rooming house poetry, its tragic drunks, and comic absurdity. Soon, it became clear to me that Gary was powering his endless bender with crystal as I'd get calls from him at all hours and the quality of his work began to slip badly. Still the *SD Scene* limped along for much of the nineties until Gary totally lost it and alienated all of our advertisers. I'd stopped partying with him when the nights began ending in the parking lot of the all night bowling alley with an angry crank dealer or at some crack den up on Cortez Hill. It was dire and, given my family history, I'd always been a bit leery of the hard stuff. The last time I saw Gary, he'd moved into an apartment in City Heights that he shared with a couple of tweekers who worked for UPS. He hadn't slept in two days and he'd lost twenty pounds. They were all sitting on a big couch in the living room with the blinds drawn at midday, the room lit only by the eerie glow of a muted TV recycling through cable news.

Gary ended up moving to Las Vegas to get a job in a casino, and the *SD Scene* went bust. I floated around for a while, living off my feeble savings until I got a job as a doorman at Molly's. Later I heard that Gary had found religion. Who knows? I, on the other hand, spent my time listening to stories of longing and despair, or reading the newspaper on my stool by the door. One old guy would come in every night and tell me the story of his son, a vet, who he claimed looked just like me. The son had come home from Nam, become a cop, and killed himself out of the blue one night, leaving a family behind. He'd tell me the story every evening, in the same way, as if I'd never heard it before. I'd sit patiently and watch as his eyes got teary and wait for him to pat me on the shoulder before he shouldered up to the bar for his first drink. Sometimes I'd carry him back on my shoulder to the Arlington, where he had a room, knock on the door, and hand him off to the woman at the front desk. Other than that, I just had to make sure that Dee Dee, the hooker who worked the bar, didn't turn tricks in the bathroom. The rest was checking the occasional ID when the sailors came by for a snort before looking for love at one of the dance clubs down the street.

The only real danger I encountered in my lost years at Molly's happened when I had to tackle a deranged street person who came in and waved a knife at Sally, the bartender, when she refused to serve him. I had been back in the can when I heard Sally yell my name, and I ran out and went for him like a return man from my days at Our Lady of the Sorrows. I knocked him cold and the cops came to drag him off. The next night, the fellow's friend came by, picked up the doorstop and threw it at my head. He missed and hit the jukebox. I got him in a bear hug and walked him out to the street. Later that night, I heard he got stabbed in a back alley off Market Street. His friend did a brief stint in jail and he was back out on the street. I'd see him wandering the abandoned parking lot off the corner weaving through the sea of pipeheads with his sleeping bag slung over his shoulder. It was like that, a steady stream of tragic tales from the SROs, occasionally interrupted by random violence. Mostly, I was bored. I drank too much and didn't get enough sleep.

Slowly, downtown started to change, with fancy restaurants and new shops replacing the old bars and porno theaters. Then, seemingly all at once, the dam burst and the last of the strip joints was shut down, followed by dive after dive, as if it was some kind of purge. Before the hipsters bought Molly's, I spent a year shooing away tourists and gourmet diners who'd poke their heads into the bar to gawk at the old timers like they were a curiosity at a theme park. Then hipsters bought the bar and doubled the drink prices, which sent the SRO crowd out in the brave new world in search of a place to disappear. They fired Sally and me, after keeping us on for a symbolic month or two to prove to themselves that they weren't predatory gentrifiers. Sam, the other bartender, saw the writing on the wall and managed to walk away with an entire day's take before they could fire him. Good for him, I thought. After we were gone, they booked alternative bands and hired out the bar for private parties. When they failed, the hipsters were bought out by a chain restaurant, which also failed. Three or four more chains came in and out. Finally, a luxury hotel purchased the whole block, shut down two SROs and put in a five-star restaurant. The parking lot on the corner is now a fancy condominium that can't sell any units with the economy in the dumps. Poetic justice.

Anyway, my stint as a doorman reinvigorated my desire not to waste my life working for assholes, so I got my clippings together and sent them around town. That's how I wound up at the *SD Weekly*, a job I managed to hang onto for a good chunk of the nineties. The rest, I've already told you about.

When I got back from Oceanside, I wanted to get straight to my piece about Mark Sawyer, but I checked my email and there was something there from the archivist at Wayne State whom I'd contacted about Bobby Flash. He'd been nice enough to scan all the files and photos that were relevant to my inquiry, and I was pleased to see that there was quite a bit there. The first attachment was a narrative by Gus Blanco written in response to a call put out in both *Solidarity* and *Industrial Worker* for Wobblies to write up their experiences in the free speech fights for the United States Industrial Relation Commission. Apparently the I.W.W. thought the publicity would be useful, so Big Bill Haywood and Vincent St. John asked the membership to send in all reports to I.W.W. General Headquarters in Chicago so they could be sent to DC. Blanco's report was as follows:

San Diego Free Speech Fight
By Gus Blanco
Who went through the fight from start to finish

December 30th 1911: Arrive in San Diego with Bobby Flash and several I.W.W. boys from Holtville. We get a place to flop in the Stingeree and search out I.W.W. Local 13 headquarters to get the lay of the land. The Wobs there tell us they're in a fight with Spreckels on account of having organized the Mexicans on his streetcars. Some of the men look to help with that, others, myself included, look for day work to get money for food as we are low on funds and food after the trip from Holtville. Local 13 boys who don't work on the streetcars as conductors or motormen are in mill, lumber, and laundry work. They send us the right way for day work.

January 6th 1912: I speak at a street meeting at Heller's Corner to organize some of the out of work I've met drifting in and about the Stingeree. Lots of drinking and gambling in the workingmen's district to pull the last dollar out of them. AFL in town has no interest in 'em. I give my pitch, "Fellow Workers and Friends, look at Spreckels and his fat gang with all they could want and you with nothing to show for your labors! Why should you be made to feel shabby for looking like a man in search of work? Why should you have nothing while they have everything? Let me tell you fellow workers, you need to get smart and join the one big union," etc. I finish and talk to a couple a fellas and the next one gets up and starts "Fellow Workers and Friends" when some upstanding citizen, an off duty policeman I heard, drives his car, horn blaring into the middle of the row. The Wob on the soapbox tried to warn the crowd not to respond and give the police an excuse but, men being men, a number of them took offense at nearly being hit and rocked the car while some other fellas slashed the tires. Then the police came in, roughed us up a bit, and broke up the meeting.

A bunch of the boys and me took off and ran down into the Stingeree and ducked into a bar. We proceeded to drink a whiskey or two and the talk was angry talk. "Who do they think they are busting up the meeting? I'd like to get my hands on that fella, etc." Well, me and Bobby did our best to warn them about giving the cops an excuse to put 'em in the pen. What you need to do is organize a whole bunch a workers in town, we told 'em. It seemed like a good field to plough, though some lost their courage when there was no whiskey to buck them up. Me and Bobby headed up to Headquarters to report the day's events and talk with some more boys.

February 8th 1912: Spreckels's gang on the council pass an ordinance banning street speaking. We met the ban with resistance. The Socialists, AFL and some preachers join in with us to protest the ban. Wobbly girl, Laura Paine Emerson, is arrested with two other ladies and thirty-eight men. I don't get snagged that day. Most of the soapboxers don't get further than, "Fellow Workers" before they're pulled down roughly and arrested with a few smacks and kicks for good measure. The Wobs stay disciplined and keep with passive resistance. It's just the start of the fight.

February 13th 1912: Superintendent of Police John Sehon issued a roundup order for all "vagrants." The police fill four jails with close to 300 Wobs, but more boys keep coming. Headquarters pledges to send 20,000 men if that is what it takes to win this fight. We hear reports that the men in the pen are driving the jailors to their wits' end with constant singing and hollering. They feed them mush and stale bread or leave them hungry and it does not break their will. No water to drink. The guards recommend the toilet. They put up to thirty men in a cell with four hammocks. Men sleep on the steel floor. More news of police beatings in the jails as the struggle continues inside with men taken out and beaten with clubs and pistol butts. Some strangled close to death and thrown back in the cell. Men still not broken.

February 20th 1912: I meet a boatload of Wobblies coming in from San Pedro to aid in the fight. A dozen men immediately proceed to assert their right to speak. The police wade into the meeting with batons flying but I manage to get free. They arrest the men but don't take them to jail. This is the first time I hear of the vigilante terror. About twenty men were taken out to the countryside and badly beaten and told to walk North. Later I meet up with a few of these men in Los Angeles. Others were never heard from again.

March 6ᵗʰ 1912: Man arrested for selling copies of *The Labor Leader* on the street. Meanwhile, the capitalist press is raving about the threat of anarchy and lawlessness to the good people of San Diego. The *Union* praises vigilante terror and the propertied men of the town line up behind them with few exceptions.

March 15ᵗʰ 1912: A street meeting is broken up and a man arrested for singing "Out there in San Diego/Where the Western breakers beat/They're jailin' men and women/For speaking on the street."

March 20ᵗʰ 1912: Big March to protest police brutality, perhaps 4,000 people. Police have Fire Department turn hoses on the crowd, hitting one speaker directly in the face at full force. He is knocked from his feet and lost a few teeth. Others have clothes ripped from their backs by the force of the water. There are a good number of women and children in the crowd, but this does not arouse any decency in the police. A man is arrested for covering his face with an American Flag when the hose is turned on him. He is charged with defacing the national emblem.

March 22ⁿᵈ 1912: Another man arrested for selling newspapers on the street. This time it is *The Herald* whose papers were in sympathy with free speech and at odds with the forces of "law and order." There is no difference between the thugs, vigilantes, police, businessmen, lawyers, judges, the press and politicians. They are all part of the same mob. Some of them wear the badge brazenly while trampling the rights of their fellow citizens. They know only the law of the dollar and the baton. Sometime during this period, I forget when, Colonel Harris Weinstock is sent by the Governor to investigate human rights abuses. He compares San Diego to Russian tyranny. He is later threatened himself.

March 28th 1912: Michael Hoey, a sixty-five-year-old Wob, dies after being beaten and kicked in the groin many times and left untreated on the floor of a cell. Police said he had been "laying about" when the doctor visited and recommended he be treated. Laura Paine Emerson gives a stirring speech at his funeral a few days later describing Michael's death as a Martyrdom, "I have nothing to give but myself and life is not worth living when all liberty is gone." She said that Michael was not dead but was with "the infinitude of nature" with "the hosts and martyrs to the cause of progress" he stood "transfigured in form and face." It has been said that I am a hard man, but I wept at these words as did a good number of those rough customers about me.

April 11th 1912: The San Diego Chamber of Commerce goes on record publicly praising the actions of the City Council, the police, and the vigilantes.

April 15th 1912: Vigilantes meet a train of Wobblies coming into San Diego from Los Angeles and stop it, kidnapping dozens of men and forcing them to kiss the flag, sing "The Star Spangled Banner," and run the gauntlet. That evening, the editor of *The Herald* was kidnapped and threatened if he does not cease publication of his paper. He does not comply and the paper is later smuggled into the city from Los Angeles.

April 20ᵗʰ 1912: Vigilante violence at a high point with dozens of Wobs disappearing. Bobby Flash is nabbed with a bunch of boys after speaking at Heller's Corner. No word from Bobby after that point. I fear my friend and comrade has been murdered.

April 30ᵗʰ 1912: I am finally nabbed by the police who promptly hand me over to the vigilantes. They blindfold me and put me in a car for a long drive. When one of them catches me trying to raise my head, I am knocked cold by a hard club or some other weapon. I awoke as the car stopped in some hills out of the town. The men remove my blindfold and I notice one is a policeman I had seen in town, out of his uniform. They strip me down and kick me in the groin. Once I dropped to my knees, the cop lights a cigar and burns I.W.W. into my behind as I am held down by two big thugs. I refuse to sing or kiss the flag. This results in a savage beating. I was bleeding about the head but the most pain came from the rifle butt they used to break two of my ribs. I am cracked one last time on the head from behind and left for dead, but miraculously, I survived. Something to be said for a hard head, I suppose. Am found by a woman on horseback and taken to a hospital in Oceanside where I spend weeks in recovery. One nurse is kind and the other will not touch me. It is better than being dead.

May 7ᵗʰ 1912: A fellow Wobbly, Big Ben Jackson, comes to see me and passes on the news that Joe Mickolash was murdered by police, shot while trying to defend himself after taking a bullet in the leg in front of I.W.W. headquarters. We trade stories and agree that Michael and Joe are the ones to make the papers, but that many more poor bindlestiffs like us have been killed with no one to notice them gone or remember them with a fancy speech. So many of the Wobs were friendless and far from home, come to help their fellow workers, only to find the cruelty of strangers. Mickolash had a big funeral in Los Angeles that I was still too banged up to attend.

May 14th 1912: Emma Goldman comes to San Diego while I am still in the hospital. She is kept from speaking and Reitman is tortured and tarred and feathered out in the sticks by the vigilantes.

May 30th 1912: I am set loose from the hospital, still scarred and limping but alive. I hop a freight back down to San Diego. Police at the station recognize me and put me back on a train to Los Angeles with the warning, "The next time we send you back, it will be in a box."

June 10th 1912: In Los Angeles for little more than 1 week, wash a few dishes in the back of a tavern to gather some coin and rest up as my leg is still nagging me. At the I.W.W. hall I hear a funny story from a Wob just in from San Diego that the vigilantes stormed a "hobo camp" that turned out to be a group of boy scouts. They were panicky as a whole bunch of Wobs was let loose after a case of small pox hit the jail. I inquire with a bunch of fellas if they heard from Bobby Flash, my partner from Holtville, and one says he thinks he seen him a couple weeks ago heading North to San Francisco, another fella says he heard he got killed in San Diego, a third man told me he heard he headed back down to rejoin the fight. I never found out who was right as I took sick and was laid up for several weeks.

July 15th 1912: Once I finally got better, I joined up with a group of fellas heading back down to San Diego where the fight was still on. We snuck in late on a freight and made our way into the Stingeree in the early morning. I met up with some boys I remembered who told me the fight was not going well. Things had quieted down a lot but the town was still locked down and the vigilantes and police had gone so far as to threaten the Governor's special investigator, Weinstock, for telling the truth. Still they were still picking up Wobs every day even with all the big crowds gone. "One martyr a day," was how we put it. I made my way to an I.W.W. house where a group of us was looking at ways to break the stranglehold of the vigilantes. The police still remembered me so I laid low for a while, waiting to see where events would take us.

August 13th 1912: The lawyers for the Free Speech League left for Los Angeles after the Attorney General failed to get an indictment for the San Diego vigilantes. The money for their lawyers came from Spreckels and the Santa Fe Railroad.

August 22nd 1912: Six men arrested in El Cajon on suspicion of being part of a plot to dynamite the new Spreckels Theatre and other buildings in downtown San Diego. The police claimed they were also plotting another "raid" across the border. I had not heard a word of any such plot amongst the I.W.W. men in San Diego or Los Angeles.

August 23rd 1912: The I.W.W. house I had been staying at near 15th and G was raided by police. I escaped out the back having had enough of San Diego justice. The news was that a prisoner had "confessed" to a plot for "the invasion of Mexico." As with the first story, this was news to me who had been in the house and never heard tell of our plot to "capture lower California." And it surely would seem unlikely that anyone would have given it a second try so soon after the first revolt got crushed. After my escape, I headed back up to Los Angeles putting an end to my dealings in San Diego. Some say that the fight was won when Emma Goldman finally spoke unmolested in San Diego in 1915, but many a dead Wob might beg to differ. As a result of my experiences there, I have come to question the effectiveness of nonviolence as the police will pin some outrage on you whether you are timid as a mouse or fierce as a tiger. This was confirmed yet again when I went with a group of Wobs, including Frank Little, to join the fight in Denver in 1913.

So it appeared that both Blanco and Flash were picked up by the police in San Diego, but neither one of them was sent back to Holtville. Apparently the powers that be were more interested in dishing out vigilante justice than checking their records or seeing if they were operating under aliases. I was also intrigued by the possibility that Bobby Flash had been killed by the vigilantes sometime after he gave his account of the gauntlet to *The Sun*. I entertained this possibility for a few seconds until I opened the next attachment, which contained a series of photos: Bobby Flash soapboxing in Minot, North Dakota in 1913; Bobby Flash at an anti-war rally in San Francisco in 1917; Bobby Flash standing in a crowd of Wobblies in front of the I.W.W. Headquarters in Chicago, two men to the right of Big Bill Haywood, no date on the picture; Bobby Flash in a "Hobo College" sitting in a room of men and women listening to Ben Reitman, no date on the picture. It appeared that Flash had made his way out of San Diego alive and well and had continued in Wobbly circles for at least five more years, into his thirties. I thought again about my great grandfather who'd died up in San Francisco—it was another thread of possibility, however tenuous.

When I got to the next attachment, I was surprised to see a letter from Flash himself in the *Industrial Worker*, June 10th, 1911. I read on:

Letter from Lower California
By Bobby Flash, I.W.W.

Fellow workers and friends,

I know that many of you have heard it said that the poor man has no right to travel. You have seen that a man with a pocket full of money can go wherever he wants while the bindlestiffs and poor working men can be driven out of a camp at the whim of any policeman or paid thug. Well, friends, I write to tell you that we have found paradise down here in Mexico. We are living high and flying the Red Flag in Tijuana, Mexicali, Tecate, and San Quintin. Down here across the border we have a workers' Utopia. It's a new world being born inside the shell of the old. We do not work; we do not get pulled into the pen for vagrancy; we do not kneel down to any man. We are Mexicans, Indians, Americans, workers and outcasts from around the world, but we know no country.

Why would you beg for a living on the other side of the border when the fight with Diaz is being won down here? Why be pushed around from town to town, hungry and alone, when our cooperative commonwealth has thrown capitalism in the ditch here in a place of our own? We have seen workers coming in from around the country to join the fight. All hands are welcome. Come and back us up or send funds. Which side are you on, fellow workers? You can live to see the day capitalism is overthrown and men can live in peace.

Join our struggle,
Bobby Flash, I.W.W.
Under the Red Flag, Tijuana, Mexico

The last attachment was an interview with Flash that appeared to be from some kind of unpublished study on the Magónista revolt that had been donated to the archives. It was a brief, but interesting, raw transcript that just jumped into the attack at Mexicali:

I was with Leyva and Berthold when we took Mexicali in January of 1911, I think it was. Williams Stanley or Stanley Williams, was called Cohen by some of the boys but, actually, his real name was Robert Lober, was the I.W.W. man in charge of the planning at the Wob Headquarters in Holtville, just across the border. Later, Lober got shot and killed. He wasn't with us in the first raid though, just Leyva and Berthold. Anyway, the Cocopah Indians did a great job scouting out the town and finding out they didn't have any real way to defend it. So it was real easy pickings at dawn. We only killed a cop when he tried to stop us from letting loose the jailed Magónistas.

Well, we took the town and it caused a real big stir. Jack London gave a speech and declared himself "a chicken thief and a revolutionist" in solidarity with us. Emma Goldman gave a speech too in San Diego. I don't know if she called herself a chicken thief too [laughter].

In the early days there were a good number of Mexicans with us. Then there was a lot of squabbling about who was in command. Hell of a lot of yelling and cussing. Some fellas got beat up, others shot. A damn shame too because we had just won a big victory. Well anyway Leyva and Berthold got into it with Stanley as they called him at the time. We split into separate groups and I was with Stanley. When the Mexican army attacked us in the second battle at Mexicali, Stanley was killed, but we held the town. Eventually, after a few more squabbles and changes in generalissimos, Pryce took command. You'll have to pardon me but I just can't remember all the changes and names, but Pryce was an important one. He was a mercenary, but he was in sympathy with us and against Diaz, and he knew how to fight, which helps when the bullets are flying.

I never met or even saw Magón. He was in Los Angeles and never left. We got pamphlets instead of bullets from the chief revolutionary mostly. If the left could of overthrown capitalism by talking the bosses to death, we'd be living in a workers' paradise [laughter].

Anyway, eventually, Pryce, who was disobeying orders I later learned, led us West to take Tijuana. It was a fierce and bloody fight, but we took it. There were only about a thousand or so people in the town, so it wasn't like attacking a big city. We scouted the positions and attacked at dawn. A lot of people died on both sides. I never took a bullet, but I lost a few comrades on both sides of me. I was with Pryce with the main group who went straight after the town's central defenses. We may have argued a hell of a lot amongst ourselves, but we were good in a fight. We rushed the trenches and other barricades, running straight into the line of fire. Dynamite Dan had a bullet take off a chip of his ear, but he managed to get up front and take out one of their best gunners. I can't be sure if I ever hit anyone but I rushed after him blasting away and hitting the ground when I caught sight of a man aiming my way. I never had any formal training so I kind of made it up as I went along, taking whatever advice Pryce or anyone with more experience had to offer.

One thing that did bother me was the way some of the pictures of the dead ended up being sold as postcards. I saw one with one of the poor kids who'd come down from a migrant camp in the Imperial Valley to join the fight. It wasn't right, folks making money off of a man's death like that [Inaudible]. Some of the same sons of bitches that came down from San Diego to loot the town done that I'm sure. Folks like that parasite, Ferris, Spreckels's snake oil salesman.

Well, we were pretty excited at first having taken Tijuana and some of the other small border towns. It looked like we had really started something big. But slowly, we came to see that the money and re-enforcements weren't coming. Pryce opened the town up for tourists from San Diego and it got to be more like a circus side show than a revolution. I did get to meet a nice Mexican gal during that time. Patricia was her name. Real nice woman. Of course, she couldn't leave with me after the second battle, but I'm getting ahead of myself.

Anyway, Pryce fell in with Ferris and tried to drum up support for us, but that all blew up and he deserted. Ended up in Hollywood I heard. Anyway, Ferris tried to bring in his own man and turn the whole thing into a capitalist land filibuster. Some of the boys, not the Wobs, fell for it because they'd been promised land by the some of the recruiters working for Magón in Los Angeles. In any event, we almost lynched the son of bitch Ferris brought in, but decided to expel him instead and elected Mosby, a real I.W.W. man, but not a great fighter. Poor bastard got shot after the second battle when he tried to escape from the US troops who pinched him as he crossed the line.

What I remember from the second fight was how outnumbered we were, like two to one. We fought hard, but we didn't stand a chance. When the call went out for a retreat, it was every man for himself. The Mexicans who were left (a lot of them had left to fight with Madero after Leyva was deposed) took off for parts unknown as did the Indians. The mercenaries figured they'd rather surrender to the US Army. Some of the Wobblies joined 'em, but Gus Blanco and me, along with a group of the Holtville Wobs, slipped the noose and snuck across the border and made it back to Holtville without getting captured.

It didn't work out the way we wanted, but I don't regret getting caught up in the fight. Hell, it looked like we had a chance to write our own ticket for once, so what the hell? Gus and I were just beginning to get into scrapes, so this was just a warm up of sorts [laughter]. It would have been a beautiful thing, a worker's Utopia in Baja. Who knows what we could have done. The one thing I regret is leaving the loveliest woman I ever met. But that's a story for another day.

Recorded and Transcribed for *Border Revolution*, 1960.

The archivist had been nice enough to explain in his email that *Border Revolution* was a book that never came out. It was the project of a leftist historian who died before he could finish it. His son donated his father's papers to the archive. This was the only material on Flash or Blanco in the manuscript. The pictures were from a larger collection of photos of I.W.W. members and events in the archive. This was another big clue to the fate of Bobby Flash. The research for *Border Revolution* was being done in 1960, which meant that Flash would have been seventy-three years old. Was the age on the Wanted poster correct? Where was the interview conducted? Was it San Francisco? I called the archivist in Detroit. He didn't know. He did though, tell me to try both the Library for Progressive Research in Los Angeles and a private library and bookstore in San Francisco that specialized in the history of the American left and countercultures, the People's Archive. I thanked him, hung up, and wrote down the contact information.

It was late and I was too tired and distracted to start my piece on the dead Marine. I printed up the material from Wayne State, put it in a separate folder, and looked around the office. It was empty and dead silent. Neville had come and gone without saying a word to me. I sat at my desk for a moment and thought about the seventy-three-year-old Bobby Flash, recalling the story of his failed revolution and lost love. How long did Bobby Flash live after that interview? Did he die a lonely old man or in the bosom of his loving family? And what about Gus Blanco? Where did he end up after Denver? What a thrilling and horrifying ride those two had—revolutionaries, outlaws, political prisoners, martyrs, heroes, common men, lost to history. And I was on their trails, tracing the distant threads of their lives, chasing their ghosts across time.

5

The next day I stayed home and spent several hours writing the piece about Jake Sullivan, the dead Marine. It was a compelling story, but my head wasn't in it, which made the work hard and unsatisfying. Finally, I hit on what I thought was a good angle and knocked it out. When I headed into the office to talk to Neville, he took a long time to read the piece and finally looked up, frowned and said, "It's not your best work, but we'll run it."

"Thanks," I said sarcastically. He didn't respond. Instead, he pulled out a letter he'd gotten from a reader about a colony of anarchist punks living out in the desert and flipped it across his desk at me.

"Maybe this will be more up your alley," he said with a smirk. I looked over the letter, which included directions and a little hand-drawn map. It seemed like a hoax to me, and the drive would take up an entire day there and back.

"Do I get an expense account for this one? Gas, food, and lodging?" I asked without any hope of a positive response.

"Fuck no," he said and laughed.

"See you in a couple days," I replied ruefully and I grabbed my satchel and headed down the stairs toward my car. Out on 5th, the meter had expired and I had a parking ticket. I got in and tossed the ticket on the passenger's seat and flopped my stuff on top of it. It was too late to go out to the desert that day so I hit the 5 and drove up to UCSD to look over the dissertations that the archivist at the historical society had told me about. The early afternoon traffic was light and I got to the campus quickly and parked in a student lot near the library, assuring myself of another ticket, a couple more of which would consume most of my meager paycheck. This was why Hank needed to stay in college, I thought. The students all looked joyless, inwardly focused and stressed out over midterms or loans or diminished expectations. It was a long way from *Animal House*. I thought of Hank and hoped he would endure his boredom and follow through where I had faltered.

Inside the spaceship amidst the eucalyptus trees that was the library, a nice, petite blond woman wearing a Rosie the Riveter button helped me find the relevant dissertations and theses. "Great topic," she said as she sent me on my way. I settled down in a private little nook to peruse them. Most offered up the same information I'd found in other books, and none of them had any specific references to Bobby Flash. I learned a tad more about the identities of the vigilantes and their connections to the town's elite. I read a good summary of the character of the turn of the century Stingeree and the efforts to stamp out vice, which pushed the gambling and prostitution across the border where Spreckels's interests also controlled the action. There was even a famous "hole in the fence" that celebrities from Hollywood used to go to drink and gamble during prohibition. Not much else about the Magónista revolt, but I did find some interesting stuff on Communist organizers in the Imperial Valley in the 1930s. Dorothy Healey had been out there organizing workers. The whole Valley turned into a Fascist police state of sorts, just as bad as the ugliness in the teens. But that was off topic.

Finally, I checked an index in another study of the Wobblies and found a reference to Gus Blanco. It turns out he was killed in the free speech fight in Everett, Washington in 1916 after he wrote the account of the San Diego fight for the government commission. This time, however, he'd gone down fighting, as a footnote described him as a Wobbly who pulled a gun on an approaching gang of vigilantes. I guess he figured he'd rather die on his feet, than get lynched or tortured to death. Can't say I blamed him. As with most of the murders of Wobblies, nobody was ever prosecuted. Instead, the government went after them a few years after Everett, passing criminal syndicalism laws at the state and federal levels that essentially made it illegal to be a member of the I.W.W. The Feds then got the go-ahead to round up Wobblies for being Wobblies. Scores of them served long hard sentences handed down during the first Red Scare. It all reminded me of McCarthyism in the fifties and the whole hysteria after 9/11 with the Patriot Act and Total Information Awareness and people rushing to throw away their civil liberties in exchange for "safety." A whole century of bullshit. Fear was a powerful thing, I thought, and frightened people can and will do anything. With that pleasant thought, I was done for the day. I left the lifeless stacks feeling strangely sad, mourning the death of a man I never knew who went down almost a century ago fighting a losing battle.

The next morning, I packed up a bag with a toothbrush and a change of clothes, checked the oil and water in the old Mustang and hit the 5 North to the 8 and headed east against the flood of stop-and-go traffic. After a bit I was climbing up toward the Cuyamacas. I put on a Leonard Cohen mix that Hank had burned for me and lost myself in the "Tower of Song." As I left the last of the exurbs, the lunar landscape of giant boulders mixed well with a Rufus Wainright cover of "Hallelujah" and I found myself so deep into the music that I forgot everything. It was a moment of pure joy, the kind I almost thought I wasn't capable of anymore. Who would have guessed it would hit me on the I-8? During a second version of "Tower of Song," U2's backup music had me feeling positively messianic until the CD ended.

I saw the sign for the Desert View Tower and realized I was getting hungry, so I pulled off the Interstate and drove down a brief stretch of side road until I arrived at the site of the funky landmark, a 70-foot lighthouse-like lookout that stood a good 3,000 feet above the desert floor. It was painstakingly crafted, between 1923 and 1928, out of local rock by a man named Bert Vaughn. He'd meant the tower to be a tribute to the pre-highway days of America when the trek from San Diego to Yuma was an arduous journey filled with peril. I parked the Mustang and got out, glancing over at the Boulder Garden, a menagerie of skulls, buffalos, Indian heads, frogs, and folk creatures carved out of the native stone by an unemployed engineer and folk artist in the thirties. Inside the tower, an eccentric man in a coonskin cap greeted me. I paid the two-dollar entrance fee, bought a coke and a candy bar, and went upstairs to check out the view. It was still early so I was the only one climbing the spiral staircase and, once on top, I stood for a moment and gazed down across the desert at the Salton Sea shimmering in the distance.

Back on the freeway, I popped in a Slab City CD that one of the music reporters had given me for the drive. Slab City was a Mexican hardcore punk band from the Imperial Valley. It was the kind of music that made your pulse rate rise—ugly, thrashing, torta rock. I listened to "Wolf Boy Down El Dorado," "Caguama Rama," and "Milwaukee's Beast" as I hit the peak of the mountain. The temperature gauge was holding steady, which made me breathe a sigh of relief as I began the long descent toward Ocotillo, where I got off the Interstate, filled up the gas tank and gazed out at the big empty desert. From Ocotillo, I took a small highway through the desert outposts of Plaster City and Seeley before I reached El Centro in the heart of the Imperial Valley farm country. In El Centro, I turned north on 86 to Brawley where I stopped for lunch at an old diner downtown. The men in the booth next to me had cowboy hats on and the waitress called me "honey." Outside by the park, a group of migrant workers were eating bag lunches and listening to a Mexican radio station. From Brawley, I took 111 North to Niland, just off the southern tip of the Salton Sea, and turned onto Main Street East on my way to Slab City. The whole of the Imperial Valley always struck me as a Mexican version of *The Grapes of Wrath* meeting *Deliverance*, but Slab City was another animal altogether, a world apart.

During World War II, the Marines had set up Camp Dunlop here in the broiling heat between the sea and a gunnery range. After the war, the base was abandoned, leaving behind nothing but the large concrete slabs where their huts had been. In the years that followed, the site became a Mecca of sorts for home-less squatters, outlaws, social outcasts, religious nuts, burned-out hippies, alkies, addicts, anti-government types, elderly snowbirds on fixed incomes escaping the winter in their RVs, and an odd as-sortment of others yearning to live free of the watching eye of the man. Here, amidst the slabs, boondockers lived as they wanted to—with no fees or water or power or police. It was an anarchic junkyard of human and material cast-offs. In the winter, the place drew thousands, but in the scorching heat of the summer only about 150 slabbers remained to wait out the inferno. Thank God it was January.

The first thing you encountered on your way in was Salva-tion Mountain—a huge multicolored mosaic hillside of Biblical verses crowned with a cross. It took slabber Leonard Knight years to construct this monument to the Lord out of tons of adobe and thousands of gallons of donated latex paint. Leonard's creation rose out of the earth like an apparition as I approached: "God is Love." I got out to take a look and walked up to the top for a view of the Salton Sea. Leonard was below, giving a tour to a pair of German tourists in soccer jerseys and bike shorts. I waved over to him as I got back into my car to head to Slab City, and got a wave in return. I drove by the "Welcome to Slab City" sign and cruised around trying to find the anarchists. Being the peak of the season, there were hundreds of motor homes, campers, and trailers of all sorts scattered in between abandoned buses, burned-out pick up trucks, and the occasional mound of old tires. I drove around somewhat aimlessly at first, passing a few classic silver Airstreams, a huge new motor home, and a group of campers parked in a circle. Lots of folks had set up elaborate awnings or improvised patios in front of their rigs. There were even a number of make-shift structures giving the place a semi-permanent feel: the Oasis Club; the Lizard Tree Library; a church; impromptu flea markets selling cactus, bird houses, and solar panels; the Ranch Night-club, complete with a stage and cozy seats ripped out of old buses. I made a few turns and saw an abandoned grapefruit orchard and a hot spring full of bathers. Finally, I gave up and took a look at the map that came with the letter Neville gave me. It was incon-clusive as all it showed was a spot marked "Thrasher Collective" next to a dot labeled Slab City.

I was snarling in disgust at Neville's having wasted my time on a hoax when a scruffy dude in camouflage came over and asked if he could help out. When I told him I was looking for a bunch of anarchist punks who'd formed a collective, he shook his head and said, "You mean the poop troop?" Then he proceeded to give me his version of the lowdown. Apparently, Slab City was divided between the "Suburbs" on the south side and "Poverty Flats" on the north side. The anarchists or "poop troop" were on the north side, he told me. I got out of the car and shook his calloused hand and told him I was a reporter from San Diego. This prompted him to introduce me to a crew of gruff-looking oldsters sitting in lawn chairs outside a Winnebago. They handed me a Pabst Blue

Ribbon and bid me to sit with them. From this group, I got the story that Slab City was being threatened by a bunch of dumbass litter bugs who were going to wreck the whole thing by dumping old cars, toxic waste, beer cans, and their own feces into the fragile desert ecology. These guys even had a website to support their cause.

"This place is one of the last outposts of real freedom in the United States," a leather-faced codger in a dirty cowboy hat offered up. "The government is always looking for ways to shut freedom down and these assholes are just giving them an excuse." This got a rousing round of approval from the rest of the men who explained that the authorities had occasionally made noises about clearing out Slab City or tearing down Salvation Mountain, but the town of Niland would just as soon have the slabbers around, because they spent what coin they had in Niland, which would just about dry up and blow away without them.

"We ain't against the party," one clearly drunk man in a ratty, red "Are We Having Fun Yet?" hat broke in. "We're against dumb-shits. And these poop troopers you're talking about are crapping in our front yard." It turned out that most of the anarchists were tent campers and tent campers buried their waste in the ground, but the desert climate didn't allow for their leavings to decompose quickly, so they were rapidly turning the Slabs into one big toilet, according to my new friends. The poop troop, the litterbugs, and the dumbass hillbillies who were dumping wrecks all over the place were going to kill the whole Slab City enterprise. By this time, I had finished my beer. I thanked my hosts and walked back over to my car and drove to poverty flats. On this side of Slab City, I saw fewer motor homes and more trailers, pick up trucks, and vans. While the suburbs had no doubt been full of interesting characters, the flats had a darker feel. I got a few inquiring stares and some guy in a truck with "Fuck Everyone" painted on the side, flipped me off, which only seemed appropriate. I drove by a trailer where a haggard young woman was screaming at her little boy. At another camp, a guy who looked like a biker was sitting on the back of his pickup truck, he waved so I pulled over and asked him about the anarchists, telling him about my conversation with the men in the suburbs.

"Fuckheads," he said. "If they don't watch it, they're going to wake up in a burning bed." I was a bit taken aback but I played it straight and listened. "That's the law out here, man. Fuck with me and I'll fuck with you." He went on at great length explaining how the last guy to call the cops out here had his trailer burned up. There was a long litany of guys who'd had their asses kicked, been shot, or had never been seen again. He didn't know where the anarchists were. I thanked him and moved on, passing an old school bus with flowers painted on it and glancing over at a big group of people, several families, in dirty tie-dyes, thread bare jeans, and faded sundresses. Some of them were smoking pot while the kids played beside them, another group were dancing to no music.

Finally, after driving by a pair of dune buggy corpses and the shell of an abandoned Range Rover, I spotted a VW van adorned with dozens of stickers and a pirate flag, surrounded by a circle of fraying dome tents. The driving sounds of hardcore were spilling out of the van. I parked the car and walked over to meet the anarchists. The first person I saw was a kid with an overgrown mohawk that had begun to flop over a bit. "Hey dude, welcome to the Thrasher Collective," he said without a hint of irony. I looked at him—skinny and dirty, his face badly broken out. He couldn't have been more than sixteen years old. I surveyed the other Utopians, who appeared to be a pack of scrawny teenage runaways.

They were all vegans, punk kids who had met online and decided to start a commune. They had even worked up a badly written manifesto about how they were rejecting the hypocrisy of the capitalist system and a world based on false needs. I read it and said, "cool," with my best poker face. There were a few very young girls with shaved heads that were starting to show some peach fuzz from neglect. One of the girls, a pretty-faced thirteen-year-old, had several fading bruises on her face and arms.

I sat with them and got their stories. They were indeed all runaways, all abused in some way or other. One of them had mailed out their manifesto to a few alternative newspapers and Neville had gotten interested and sent me out to Slab City without telling me much else about it. While there wasn't much of a political story here, there was a tale worth telling. I went back over to my car and grabbed my digital camera and took a picture of the group of twelve kids. They all raised their fists and said, "Power to the people" as I took the shot. I reached into my pocket and gave the kid with the mohawk a twenty. I couldn't help but think of Hank as a teenager threatening to run away from Kurt's house to ride the rails like Kerouac. The mohawk thanked me effusively. It was late afternoon by now and I wanted to check out a few more camps before I left.

I looped around the back side of poverty flats and cruised by a trailer someone had covered with found objects—shoes, plates, springs, hub caps, pieces of scrap metal, and ocotillo branches. There was a pet cemetery and a dirt golf course. I noticed that a lot of the folks out here were older women. I made my way back around to the suburbs and parked by the Lizard Tree Library. The library consisted of a pair of small shacks patched together from plywood, garden fencing, and whatever else was around. It was quite picturesque, located beside a little tree with a swing hung on the biggest branch and a nice bench right next to that. Inside, the books were neatly housed in battered old bookcases or make-shift shelves. The collection had its share of mysteries, romances, and crime novels left behind by the snowbirds, but I also saw *The Stranger* by Camus, some poetry collections, and *Do It* by Jerry Rubin side by side with a book by Rush Limbaugh. Just then, a kind-faced older woman in jeans and a flannel shirt came over.

"I hear you're writing an article," she said with no introduction. When I replied that I was, she continued, "Well, don't believe the whole suburbs versus the flats thing some folks will tell you. It's never been that clear-cut. There's a bunch of well-intentioned do-gooders that want to save us from ourselves; there's a bunch of stupid rednecks who just want to drink and raise hell and trash the place; there's some lonely old folks escaping the winters; there's a patch of hippies who keep to themselves and get stoned all day; there's the 'leave me the fuck alone crowd'; there are some bible thumpers; there are some real piece of shit criminals hiding out from the law; there are folks that live on the road; there are migrants. You get my drift?"

"Yes," I said smiling at her, "it's complicated."

"And it's a real community, believe it or not," she said earnestly. "People live and die here. They feed each other, keep each other company, take care of one another. Folks have been coming back here every fall for years. There's something special here that you can't get anywhere else. It's freedom but it's folks taking care of each other too. Don't have much of that out there in the world now do you?" I nodded my head. Her name was Erma. She invited me back to her camp where a big group of ladies, as they called themselves, and a few of their gentlemen friends had assembled around a huge fire as the sun got low and the evening chill began to settle in. They had musical instruments, two guitars and a banjo, and they began to play song after song, with the whole group joining in if they all knew the words. I sat down on a spare milk crate and listened to them sing with voices full or frail, happy or sad, depending on the singer. As the night came on, the sky to the west went from blood red to black and I heard Woody Guthrie, Hank Williams, Bob Dylan, Merle Haggard, Loretta Lynn, Jimmy Buffet, and a few songs I didn't know. Between tunes I overheard two ladies talking about going to visit the widower of a woman who'd died a few weeks back. They'd been together for thirty years. He wasn't doing that well and a cake might cheer him up a bit, the women hoped. I thought about the utter loneliness of an old man, facing unrelenting grief and then death in this cruel desert. The faces about me in the campfire light were old and battered, I noticed, but they were singing. Just then, Erma took a turn at the guitar and began to sing, "This little light of mine, I'm gonna let it shine," and I looked up into the new night sky at the tough old stars.

The next morning, I woke up in a cheap motel in Brawley still thinking about Slab City. I'd gotten into Brawley late, had trouble getting to sleep, and had one of those strange fitful nights where your dreams are full of the faces and images from the day before. So I was singing Woody Guthrie and fleeing burning trailers in God's Country all night long. In the morning, I went for coffee and breakfast at the same little diner after noticing that it was just down the street from where a farmworkers' union hall had been in the thirties. I had eggs and bacon and listened to a redneck guy bitch to the waitress about "the big nig" in the White House who was bringing Muslim Communism and baby murder to Brawley any time now. The waitress called him "honey" and told him she didn't care about politics. I finished my breakfast quickly and left.

It was early and I wanted to check the court records out in El Centro for anything on Bobby Flash before heading back. I got into town and found the records office without any problems. The clerk, who looked like an ex-linebacker with a flat top, was a bit of a history buff and was pretty excited to help me track down an outlaw from days gone by. After an intensive search that took over an hour, we found the same Wanted poster that I'd discovered in San Diego. No arrest or trial records though.

"Looks like he got away with it," the clerk said with a grin. I thanked him and headed back out to the Mustang, driving past a gigantic motorhome sales lot before I hit 8. On a whim I continued east, passed scores of farmworkers toiling in the fields, big tractors kicking up dust, and motorhomes full of snowbirds making their way to Winterhaven, Arizona. I saw the sign for Holtville, got off the Interstate, and drove through a patch of farmland until I hit what there was of Holtville. The town was centered around Holt Park by City Hall, a cream-colored, vaguely Mission-style, two-story building with arched doorways and windows. I parked the car and walked through the park and sat down on a bench by the gazebo. There was a family having a picnic at a table under a tree. I tried to imagine Bobby Flash somewhere in town; perhaps his Wanted poster had hung up on a wall in City Hall. The family started to sing "Happy Birthday" in Spanish to a beaming little girl in a white dress. A pickup loaded with hay drove down the main street, followed by flatbed full of migrant workers. I walked over to a sign in the square that explained that Holtville was founded in 1903 by W.F. Holt, who had fled Missouri for health reasons. Much of the main street and the town's theater had burned down in separate fires that had obliterated most of the Holtville of old, aside from the City Hall. There was nothing to be found here, no trace of the ghosts of the Wobblies who planned revolution or the outlaw who fled town on some-body else's horse.

6

I spent the whole next day at home, writing up the Slab City story, "Utopia on the Slabs." Before I headed down to the office, I called to see if Neville would be there and got word from one of the music writers that he was out, but that he'd be back later. I took this as a "yes" and walked down the hill to get some exercise, cutting over to E Street to check my PO box before I hit the *New Sun*. Nothing from Hank, but there was a letter from my old pal Shane, who I played football with at Our Lady of the Sorrows. We'd kept in touch and visited each other for over twenty years now. I put the letter in my back pocket and headed to the office to hand in my piece to Neville. When I got there, he still wasn't in, and neither was the music writer. I flopped a copy of the piece on Neville's desk and sat down to read the letter from Shane.

Shane had mailed the letter from Arcata, California, a college town up by the redwoods far north of San Francisco, where he had spent the last few years with an environmental group, "Redwoods Forever," working on conservation. Before that he'd had a job with the local Greens. That was what had brought him up to Arcata in the first place after he left his job in San Francisco. Now, I was surprised to learn, Shane was leaving his gig with the conservation group to move to what he called "a collective" near Petrolia off the Lost Coast Highway just south of Arcata. "There are some fantastic people down there," the letter read. "It may sound crazy, but I want to give this a chance. Why not try to live my ideas rather than just talk about them?" I thought of the teenagers out in Slab City and wondered what the hell had gotten into him. This didn't seem like something Shane would do... Or did it?

Back in high school, our days were filled with football practice and petty criminal pleasures. Sometimes we'd steal a six-pack and go drink by the railroad tracks or in an orange grove behind the mall or up in the hills above Chatsworth Park. We'd rap about philosophy or girls or both. On occasion, we'd run into some loser in his twenties or thirties, the kind of guy who likes to hang out and drink with teenagers, and get him to buy us more beer. Shane was always good at that, bullshitting us into some interesting situations. We met bikers, homeless criminals on the lamb, drug dealers, and lots of other folks who would have horrified our parents. It was kind of our secret society. Once we ran into some gangbangers by the railroad tracks and we avoided getting our asses kicked by sharing our twelve pack with them. It turned out we were all Raiders fans, so we debated the merits of Jim Plunkett and agreed that Marcus Allen was the shit. Not bad kids once it was all said and done, which probably couldn't be said of Big Mike, Shane's neighbor.

Big Mike was a grotesquely obese version of one of the fabulous furry freak brother cartoon characters with a huge mop of unkempt curly black hair and a shaggy beard. He worked for a porn video company in sales and distribution, so he had a vast catalogue of product that he'd let us watch. He was always begging us to bring over girls, maybe some cheerleaders from school, a favor we never did for him. Big Mike also had several huge aquariums full of exotic but deadly creatures, including a boa constrictor, a tarantula, and a lionfish. Big Mike was really into watching them eat their prey. When he was off on a business trip, Shane would feed his menacing little zoo in exchange for a baggie of his best pot, which we would smoke in Big Mike's skull bong while watching *Debbie Does Dallas* or some other thrilling fare. Once we lost our initial boners, we both came to the conclusion that porn was, ultimately, boring. After a few bong loads, we'd find ourselves in a fit of laughter over some inane dialogue or a ridiculous scene. Apparently, we concluded, America's sexual unconscious was a perpetual high school dirty joke. Big Mike was making a living catering to the adolescent desires of the middle-aged accountants who ran the world. Pathetic, we thought. It came as no surprise when the police showed up to take Mike away on some undisclosed crime.

Other times, after practice, when we didn't have to hit one of our many short-lived, shitty mall jobs, we'd get high and take the bus to used record stores. Before we got into our punk purist stage we'd scour the bins for old blues and jazz, sixties psychedelia, and promo copies of new music. At one point, we really dug The Doors. We found all their albums in pretty short order, but then we discovered a cool shop over the hill in Hollywood that sold bootlegs. I got a tape of the Miami Concert where Jim Morrison was arrested, a soundboard copy of *American Prayer* with a bunch of unreleased poems, and a concert where Morrison was on acid. We got so into The Doors that we both read a Jim Morrison biography and followed it up by going to the library and checking out all the books that Jim had read: William Blake's *Marriage of Heaven and Hell*, Friedrich Nietzsche's *Birth of a Tragedy*, Jack Kerouac's *On the Road*, Norman O. Brown's *Life Against Death*, and Aldous Huxley's *The Doors of Perception*. I could quote the line from Blake where The Doors' name came from, and Shane started dropping words like "Dionysian." We didn't get it all completely, but it was heady stuff for the back of the bus.

When Shane found out that Ray Manzarek, The Doors' old keyboardist, had produced the first X album, we were all over it. Shane, who'd just gotten a car, made his way over to the Whiskey to see X live and that was the beginning of our identity as punks.

I remember the first time he took me with him and I stood in the back of the crowd as the band went into a searing version of "Los Angeles," and the thought of watching them on the same stage where Morrison had done his first version of "The End" was thrilling beyond words. It was like nothing in my life up to that point. I felt the energy surging through the crowd as they fed off of Billy Zoom's rapid-fire guitar riffs and John Doe's and Exene's dissonantly beautiful harmonies. They did "We're Desperate," and the whole crowd sang along with "My whole fucking life is a wreck." Something was really happening, I thought.

Then there was the time Shane scored some acid from some guy we met in the park. We thought we were pretty clever so we read up on it before we decided to do it, devouring *The Electric Kool Aid Acid Test*, *Fear and Loathing in Las Vegas*, and *Centre of the Cyclone* to make sure we were prepared to embark on our inner journey. In any event, we determined we'd take it one Friday night at the movies. The Nuart was showing The Who movies *The Kids are Alright* and *Quadrophenia*, which seemed appropriate at the time for some reason. I remember sitting in the dark theater waiting for the light show to start for what seemed like a long time, until, slowly, the edges of everything rounded, and the quality of sound changed dramatically. It was as if I was hearing inside of the music, note by note. Pete Townsend's guitar chords exploded in my head like the Fourth of July and Roger Daltrey's voice surrounded me completely. During one scene, Daltrey appeared to be walking through a luminescent corridor of some sort. I leaned over to Shane and said, "Roger Daltrey is Jesus" and we both almost peed our pants laughing. As the acid got stronger, I was struck by a feeling of overpowering joy in the wake of the laughter. Everything was simply oceanic—and then the first film ended.

I tried to speak to Shane but he was sitting with his eyes closed, smiling, lost somewhere in the distant recesses of his being. Stupidly, I got up to go to the bathroom. During the intermission, what was a half-full theater had been invaded by an army of Mods and Rockers. I glanced outside at the street and spied a myriad of shiny new Vespas by the curb. They were rich Westside kids, rude and full of pretensions, and their dress up and play scene would have usually filled me with disgust. A gang of them were barking orders at the beleaguered kid at the popcorn stand, mocking him as he filled their orders. As I stood behind a line of trench coats in the men's room I became unhinged. Literally, I was just in line to pee, but inside I became totally disassociated, utterly gone. I couldn't remember my name or Shane's name, or what I was here to do. In the full grip of the panic, I turned around and brushed by one of the trench coats who pushed me in the back and told me to fuck off. It was as if it had happened to a different person. I just wandered into the lobby and stared in horror at the faces of the kids as their flesh fell from them and they became formless. Somehow, I made my way back inside the theater where I found Shane, still grinning with his eyes closed. I sat in my seat, the lights went down, and the film began and the formlessness continued now in sound as well as matter. Then I stopped hearing altogether, and I closed my eyes, terrified at this latest development. Behind my eyes, the world emptied out and I'm not quite sure how to describe this except to say that I saw the hollow core of the world of lies, the vacuum at the heart of all that is. And this wasn't some nice Buddhist notion; this was a big ugly nothing, a huge, looming, menacing meaninglessness. I think I wept, but I can't say for sure.

Slowly as the film dragged on, my angst began to ebb and I noticed that Shane had put his hand on my arm to calm me. As

FLASH

things began to take shape, I got a grip and started to focus on the music. What brought me back to my body and the world was the rage and sorrow in Daltrey's voice as he wailed out "Doctor Jimmy," and by the time the film ended with "Love Reign O'er Me," I felt like a prize fighter who'd lost but not been knocked out through sixteen rounds. We walked outside and headed down the street for a Coke at a diner. The high had ebbed but I was still a little wary of what else might be lurking in the back alley of my consciousness, so I was silent. Shane kept asking me if I was OK, and I just nodded. He was ecstatic, going on about how he forgot himself and thought he was seeing into the heart of matter—and it danced! Atoms dance, he told me. It was a struggle for him to put it into words but the essence of his experience was that everything in the world was interrelated, interpenetrating, all part of some big fluid common ocean of Big Self. "Everything is always alright," he kept saying as if it were profound. In an hour or so I found the words to tell him about my nightmare. He was crestfallen and kept apologizing to me even after I told him that it wasn't his fault. It was the first and last time I did acid. One dark night of the soul was enough.

Looking back on it, I think that night epitomized the difference between Shane and me. He was always sure that something better was right around the corner and I had to fight the notion that the worst was waiting for me somewhere, so I'd better watch my back. He was in love with the world and I was a spurned lover. It wasn't that Shane was super naïve or anything, it was just that he had a sense of urgent possibility. I fed on his exuberance and lust for life. He checked my anger and pessimism. What was I to him? Loyal, I suppose, and honest. Later, when he was at UCLA, he'd refer back to our different reactions to the acid and say something like, "I'm Whitman and you're Melville," or "You're an Existentialist and I'm a Taoist." One time he told me I'd had "a *Heart of Darkness* trip." It was just whatever shit was on his reading list that week, but I guess there was some truth to it. Actually there was probably a lot of truth to it.

By the time he was in his junior year, he got really political. He had this Marixist sociology professor who inspired him to want to change the world. We'd meet for coffee and he'd have some big pronouncement about "economics not culture being the driver of social change." He'd take me to political meetings at Midnight Special Bookstore in Santa Monica and buy me books about urban space and class. He joined the International Socialists and went to protests against apartheid in South Africa or police brutality in LA. I got some good leads for stories from him. By that time I'd gotten a full-time gig with the paper and had stopped taking classes at Valley College. I'd moved over the hill to Venice and was in the thick of things, or so I thought. Once in a while Shane would try to get me to go back to school. "You're smarter than most of the people in my classes," he'd say. I didn't listen.

It was around that same time that Shane got into the Grateful Dead. One of his college buddies, Josh, had toured with them and had thousands of bootlegs. At first I was very skeptical, given my allegiance to punk and my father's sad history, but I went to some shows with Shane and Josh in Ventura and I liked it. We camped for the weekend and hung out and wandered around the campground. There were lots of old hippies who traveled with the band and we talked to some of them. One guy had gone on every tour for the last twenty years. Amazing. It turns out he lived in a commune (they still existed, I learned) up in Northern California. It sounded cool, but a little flaky. I was convinced he had to be rich. "Don't be so cynical," Shane chided me. At the show the next day, Shane and Josh did some mushrooms, but I stuck to pot, still leery of my dark interior life. The show was in a rodeo arena at the Ventura Fairgrounds. They did "I Know You Rider," and the whole crowd went wild when a train went by just as Jerry Garcia sang, "I wish I was a rider, on a north bound train." I thought about the fact that the Dead were born out of the era of the first acid tests and that Neal Cassady drove the bus—the same Neal Cassady who was Sal Paradise's pal in *On the Road*. Very cool, I thought, even if the dancing was a little spastic. I liked the open-ended nature of the jamming, like jazz improvisation.

After the show, we went swimming in the ocean by the campsite. Shane talked about reading that subatomic particles weren't really separate entities but actually came together in what he called, "a fluid event." He was the only person I knew who said things like that who didn't make them sound contrived.

"Fucking hippie," I joked. He was still pretty high and laughed and then said something about how punk and hippie were just different sides of the same avant garde, countercultural coin. Just people trying to imagine some space "outside." He said "outside" in a way that was supposed to convey great meaning. I wondered about it, less sure of myself as always.

"Earth to Shane," I said, "you're full of shit." He laughed and dove under a wave. I felt a little outside not being on mushrooms with them and a bit like a coward for being afraid to get back on the horse. Shane never pushed me, though; he said that people should never do "sacred things for small reasons." I wasn't sure what that meant, but I knew that one glimpse into the void was all I needed. Later that day, I decided to interview a few hippies for an article. What I discovered was that the campgrounds across the country had been infiltrated by DEA agents posing as deadheads. They were busting kids for selling acid and sending them to prison for long terms based on minimum sentencing laws designed to go after gang members. I called the piece, "Busted down on Bourbon Street" lifting the title from the Dead's song "Truckin'."

After he graduated from college, Shane had a kind of nomadic period. He followed the Dead for a few months with Josh and then took a trip to Ecuador where he did an internship with an anti-poverty organization that was working with indigenous groups in South America. He sent me long letters about how amazing the Andes were and how great it was to wake up in an Indian village at dawn and spend the day doing "the real work" as he called it. He was "learning from the wisdom of the people," he'd write. Sometimes, he'd include a photo from some big protest in Quito or a slum in Guayaquil. After a couple months, he met a beautiful French woman at a café in Cuenca and sent me her picture too. She was a stunning beauty with raven hair, big blue eyes, and a sexy, world-weary expression on her face as she refused to smile for the camera. After his internship was over, Shane and Monique spent a few weeks in a rented flat in Baños, under a volcano at the cusp of the Amazon jungle. It was like he was playing Albert Finney playing Malcolm Lowry with Jacqueline Bisset or something. I have to admit, I was pretty damn jealous. I thought he'd never come back.

When he did, it was without the French girl, who'd returned to Europe to be exotic and beautiful there. Much to my surprise, my friend, the world traveler and international lover, got a job working for a community organization in Oakland. Before he left Los Angeles for the Bay Area, we went to a Raiders game together. We got to the LA Coliseum early and had a couple of beers in the car while we listened to "The New World" by X and chatted about the future.

"You know, you're my best friend in the world," he told me. We toasted our friendship and his new job and pledged to stay in touch. When I told him how proud I was of all the stuff he'd done and what he was about to do he surprised me.

"I've got nothing on you, man. You're something special. You're a self-taught, self-made man. And you're a fearless motherfucker too." I asked him what he meant by fearless.

"You stare the world right in the face," he answered. "That takes courage."

"Thanks, man," I said and hugged him. I'd never known that he felt that kind of respect for me before, but it was just like him to say a kind thing at the right time. I loved him for it. We finished our beers and got out of the car to wade through the crowd. A Raiders game is like a Dead show with *carne asada* instead of veggie burritos, beer instead of acid, and, of course, bloodlust for football rather than psychedelic music. Still the crowds were similar in that both came in costume and expressed a kind of longing for community and fellow feeling. It didn't matter if you were white, black, brown, or yellow—it was all about the silver and black. We shared a few high fives and back slaps with our fellow fans and headed in to our seats. We were way up top in the last row and could see the downtown LA skyline if we looked behind us. It was a good game, but the Raiders fell to the Broncos on a bad call in the fourth quarter and that was all it took to flip the switch. We could see the fights breaking out as bodies flew and the crowd moved in ripples below us. The cops arrived in force, as they always did, with riot gear on, and the mood turned ugly fast. The teams had left for the locker room and the crowd below us was chanting, "Fuck the police." It was too bad. I'd been hoping to get a win on the day my best friend left town for good.

Up in Oakland, Shane helped at-risk kids get jobs, tutoring, and other social services. His office was in East Oakland where they'd lost not just the Raiders but thousands of industrial jobs and this had torn the working class "flats" apart. East Oakland had been a refuge where people from West Oakland moved to escape violence, but now it was just as bad. There just weren't any pockets of peace left in the flats. The hills were a different story with big houses and plenty of services. Down in the flats, there were neighborhoods with no grocery stores, no banks, nothing but fast-food joints and liquor stores. Crack was hitting big too and people were getting shot every day it seemed. At first, Shane lived downtown in a loft space with some artists and his letters were full of enthusiasm for the "poetry of the streets" amidst the economic deprivation and violence. "The drive down East 14th Street as it turns into International Boulevard is a mosaic of America—Mexican, Salvadoran, Vietnamese, African—taco stands and auto body shops, the anarchy and play of the streets, mean and beautiful," he wrote once. I could tell the place had really gotten into his blood and he loved it. He worked long hours with kids from Elmhurst who had to run away from gangs on their way to and from school. One time he sent me a picture of one little boy, Roy, whose mother had been murdered by a drug dealer. Roy was living with an aunt who worked the night shift as a janitor and had to sleep in the day. He was a cute little guy with a sweet smile who ate up the attention he was getting from the white boy at the outreach center. Then, the letters stopped coming as frequently.

When I finally did get another in a month or so, it was postmarked from San Francisco. It turned out that little Roy had been killed by stray gunfire in his Elmhurst neighborhood. They never caught the gunman because the neighbors were too scared to testify. It was "horrible beyond words," Shane wrote. He'd moved across the bay to a place in the Mission so he had a "refuge" from work. He kept at it for a few more years, but the poetry was gone from his letters. He'd tell me about some new project, but his tone was matter of fact, sometimes depressed even. "Another attempt to save the world went to hell this week," one of his letters started. When yet another kid he was working with died by gunfire he thought about quitting, but he stuck with it. My son would have said that he was fighting his "storm inside." Things had always seemed to come easily for Shane, but now I saw that he was really fighting the darkness. I admired that about him. He dug in and kept pushing.

Shane started saying stuff like "pessimism of the intellect, optimism of the will" and "hope is a moral obligation." It was like he was searching for some new philosophical framework to help him get through the day. When they finally had to lay him off because of budget cuts, it was probably a relief. He got another job in San Francisco pretty quickly, this one in a workers' information center that was sponsored by a group of local labor unions. The job was to help non-union workers find out what their rights were and what benefits were available for injured or unemployed workers. Real hands-on stuff.

I came up to visit him a few times when he was living in San Francisco, and we had a great time. Of course, I had to do the usual things like go to City Lights Bookstore and drink in the bars where Kerouac drank in North Beach, but we also spent a lot of time with Shane's friends in the Mission. He'd met a bunch of artists and activists who shared a big loft complex. They were good people and there was lots of stirring talk. Shane always found people like that, wherever he was. During one visit around New Years we went to a party at a loft where everybody was doing ecstasy. It wasn't like a rave with lots of bad loud disco and teenagers jumping up and down with pacifiers in their mouths. Here people were just lying around on big couches and rapping about things. I did some and it was nothing like the acid trip. I got the oceanic thing going and Shane and I talked about how much we loved each other. You get really empathetic on the stuff. It was earnest and good. I met a great woman too, a mural artist named Carla who I ended up seeing for a while, whenever I could make it up to see Shane. I remember they had "A Love Supreme" on the stereo. Toward the end of the night, a bunch of us went up on the roof and stared at the downtown skyline, sparkling like a diamond in the distance. Carla kissed me for the first time up there and I fell into her completely in the womb-like darkness. It was really something, a perfect moment.

Well, it was great for a while, going up to visit Shane and seeing Carla. Then Carla got a chance to work on a big project in New York City and Shane lost his job with the Workers' Center when the unions who were sponsoring it got into a battle about something and the whole thing fell apart. Shane had liked that work and was pretty bummed when everything crapped out. He ended up doing some odd jobs here and there and looking for more work doing activist stuff, but paying jobs were few and far between. Shane had a period of about six years where he'd get a job, get his feet wet, and then be told the money had dried up for his position. By the time I was working for the *SD Weekly,* just after the millennium, Shane had worked for two more unions, an anti-sweatshop group, a human rights organization, an anti-globalization group, and a coalition of anti-war groups just after 9/11 and in the lead up to the war in Iraq. That was the thing about San Francisco: even during the peak of the Bush years, there was still plenty of left activism. I used to tease Shane that he needed to move back to So Cal and work in the belly of the beast for a while, be a commie in San Diego for a change. He'd laugh and say, "You've got that front covered." Truth be told, I think he was pretty comfortable in his little cocoon up there in the People's Republic of San Francisco.

In any event, he finally got sick of bouncing around in the city and took what he thought was a durable, long-term gig up in Arcata. The Green Party had won the elections there and they had an opening for an organizer. So Shane packed up and moved to Arcata only to find out that the job with the Greens wasn't any more stable than the hit-and-miss gigs he'd been getting in San Francisco. He fell in love with the area, though, and decided to stay. It turns out the great outdoors was a welcome respite from the city. He told me, "It helps me get in touch with something bigger." More "big self" stuff, but this time there was no acid involved. I came up to visit him and he took me all over the place, hiking through redwood forests, fishing on the Pacific with some cool redneck dude he'd met. He even took up surfing in the icy water near Patrick's Point. I preferred to sit on the cliff in my jacket and watch, keeping a lookout for shark fins. "What if they think you're a seal?" I'd tease him. Nonetheless, he seemed happy.

I'd lost track of him for a few months before the letter about the collective, so it seemed to come out of the blue. But, when I thought about it, it did seem to make sense. Shane was always searching for something, really. Even during his darkest days in Oakland, he never totally lost his sense of the possible. I just hoped this wasn't going to be a disaster. We'd both spent our lives doing whatever we wanted, not worrying about security or savings or health insurance, or any of that. "Death on the installment plan" was what Shane called it. But moving out to some commune in his early forties did seem a little reckless, I thought, even for him. Sooner or later, we were going to have to face reality. We were getting older. What the fuck was Shane doing?

Neville loved the Slab City piece and we got a good response from readers on the article I did on the Marine, so it seemed like a good time to cash in and take my week off so I could head up to LA, see Hank, and follow up on Bobby Flash at the Library for Progressive Research. I left early on a Friday, but it didn't matter and I still got stuck in inexplicable wall-to-wall traffic on the 5 as soon as I got past Camp Pendleton. I looked at the people around me, trapped in their cars, plugged into their various devices. The way people talked into their handless phones made them look like crazy street people talking to themselves. When the traffic did move it sped up to sixty or seventy and then screeched to a halt. There was a frustrated, arrested quality to the movement. I remembered back in my LA days walking downtown around rush hour and glancing down at the freeway intersections from the top of an overpass, marveling at the insanity of it all—the ecological disaster of it, the millions of hours of wasted time, the myriad of heart attacks and ulcers in the making, and the blood red sunsets from the smog. Sometimes, I liked to look back at the eyes of the driver behind me in the rearview mirror. There was a strange intimacy in the act; it was like fishing for humanity amidst the mass of checked-out car zombies. I got flipped off a couple times doing it. People think they can do anything behind the wheel and there's more murder than mercy in the air on the Interstate.

After a long hard slog, I hit the 110 and the traffic picked up as I cruised toward South Central. I got off at Gage and drove to Vermont and found the library. In the lobby there were posters advertising an upcoming lecture by a former Black Panther and the debut performance of a play by a lesbian Chicana theater troupe. I found the librarian, a gray-haired African-American woman wearing rimless glasses and a bright red Che Guevera t-shirt, and told her what I was looking for before she disappeared behind a monitor for a moment. She re-emerged with two possibilities. There wasn't anything on the San Diego free speech fight, but there was a file with a couple of references to San Diego Communist Party members and some things on the Llano colony that might have some references to the I.W.W. The first thing I checked was the file on the Communist Party, no luck there. There was a lot of interesting material on a strike in the Imperial Valley and something about Luisa Moreno organizing cannery workers on the waterfront in the thirties, but nothing going back to the free speech fight. I sighed. It was a long hard drive to get shut out. I was not very optimistic about the Llano section, but I did take some time to look over the books and magazines they had on the subject.

All the material noted that the Llano Colony was born out of the ruins of Socialist Los Angeles. After years of intensifying labor conflict between local unionists of all stripes and the *Los Angeles Times* owner and self-appointed petty despot of LA, General Otis, everything came to a head when the McNamara brothers, two AFL unionists, were arrested for dynamiting the *Times* building. Holy shit! Interestingly, the same crooked cop who had nabbed Flores Magón found the bombs at the *Times* building. It figured, I thought. Anyway, the McNamaras' trial and the mayoral contest, in which Socialist Job Harriman was widely expected to win, polarized the city. On the one side, Otis and his allies wanted to keep Los Angeles an open shop town with an abundance of cheap labor, while on the other side, Harrimen and the workingmen of Los Angeles were looking to break Otis's stranglehold on the city and push for public ownership, union shops, and bottom-up democracy. It was a battle for the soul and future of Los Angeles. Everything was looking up for Harriman until, just days before the election, the McNamaras confessed and Harriman's mayoral bid went up in flames. Bummer. The loss set the labor movement in Los Angeles back for decades. Now the owners made the rules. It was the plot of a film noir movie where the bad guy wins.

It reminded me of the movie *Chinatown* and I kept reading. Apparently, in the wake of his devastating loss, Harriman had decided to "retreat to the desert" and start a co-operative colony that could serve as an experimental model of a socialist society. "In the heart of every man is the instinctive desire to get on the land," Harriman wrote. I thought of Shane and read on, looking at a map that showed the location of Llano, twenty miles from Palmdale in the Antelope Valley. At the time it had been a barren desert, but within a year over 300 colonists were living there, with thousands of visitors coming every year. The original group were all from Harriman's circle, but word soon spread in *Western Comrade, Llano Colonist*, and elsewhere, and socialists, Wobblies, and utopians of various other stripes flooded into Llano. I looked at an old black-and-white picture of the hotel clubhouse made of wood and native stone and a line of adobe stone cabins that housed the inhabitants. At its peak, Llano had a printing press, seventy acres of gardens, a machine shop, a rabbit and poultry farm, a boot shop, a laundry, a dairy, bee keepers, cabinet makers, a fish hatchery, a saw mill, a soap factory, a huge orchard, hundreds of acres of alfalfa, and dozens of other "departments." It was the biggest, most successful communal experiment west of the

Mississippi. They even had an arts studio, literary programs, musical events, and the first Montessori school. And these commies liked sports! They had a championship baseball team, a football team, and more. I laughed to myself. Impressive—I'd heard of the place but I didn't know it had been so big.

Of course, it had its enemies from the beginning with Otis and his crew sending in spies and provocateurs to mess with Harriman. It wasn't enough to win an election; they had to totally discredit the guy, run him out of the region. So Llano, it turned out, was "democracy with the lid off" as one frustrated colonist put it. Colonists squabbled over work, planning, the decision-making process, and everything else you could think of that would start an argument. Harriman was dragged into court, and the LA papers ridiculed his project on a regular basis. Go figure. Still the thing survived and kept growing for a few years, until Harriman discovered that they didn't have enough water to sustain Llano's growth and decided to move the colony to Louisiana, where it survived into the thirties. I looked over a few more pictures in the middle of the book. What struck me most was the incredible social life of the place. They had parades on May Day, concerts, and plenty of visitors despite the hard work of building their dream in the desert.

The next thing I looked over was a bound collection of old copies of *Western Comrade* and *Llano Colonist*. I was absentmindedly skimming through the pages when something stopped me in my tracks. It was a photo of the Llano Sluggers baseball team with the names listed below. There in the second row of players was "Bobby Flash, shortstop." I pored over the rest of the piece and there was nothing else but the picture. Still, my interest was piqued and I surveyed every other thing on the shelf until I found an old hardcover book, entitled *Llano Days*, published in the mid-fifties on some obscure press. It had interviews with former colonists and one of them was Bobby Flash:

> I was there in Llano for a patch in 1915 and back a couple more times in later years before they moved down south. Llano was set up by Job Harriman and some Socialists from Los Angeles after they lost the big election around the time of the *Times* bombing which was a frame job if you ask me. Well, in any event, there were a good number of Wobblies who passed through Llano along with me. Some folks described it as hard living, but for a Wob, having a place to hang your hat is home.
>
> There was one fella there, Gibbons, who said he was a Wob, but I'd never met him before Llano. Well, this Gibbons gave us all a bad name by talking up a storm about the One Big Union and the cooperative commonwealth of all the workers in the clubhouse and then takin' sick or claiming to have some mystery injury in his back or leg or some such place. If the work required bending over, it was his back. If it required walking a bit, his leg would be bothering him. Folks got to callin' it "Gibbonitis" when somebody slacked on a job. Now I never had any problem with a fella putting on the wooden shoe on the job to get at the bosses, but this was other workers he was shamming. So I didn't have much to do with that so-called Wob.
>
> Some of the other boys I knew from the sidecars or soapboxes showed up and put in their share of work. It was a beautiful thing they built there and I'd have to say that my time there was some of the best days of my life. You could really see what folks working together (for each other and not the bosses) could do. Sure there was a good deal of squabbling in the General Assembly, but most of the folks were more interested in the work of the colony. We had fields for as far as the eye could

see and farm animals that we raised and slaughtered ourselves. We lived by the products of our own labor and didn't hand over the profits to some parasite. I worked washing dishes in the kitchen, helped with hauling rocks to the construction sites, and lent a hand at harvest time. It was good work. We were really building something—a model of what folks could do outside of capitalism.

They also had schools there at Llano. For the little ones, they built the first Montessori school in the country. But they had schools for adults too, which I took advantage of many evenings. We'd talk about different theories of Socialism or talk about some poem by Walt Whitman or a passage in Thoreau. My mother had been a schoolteacher so I was raised reading and writing, but after she died I was never able to finish school, so, being mostly self-taught, I enjoyed the opportunity to talk with folks and try on a new idea or two. I remember a quote by Thoreau that we discussed one evening, about how "the mass of men lead lives of quiet desperation." This was, I thought, what my whole life had been about—not giving up or being resigned to taking it. We had a real good talk about this quote I remember and it stuck with me. The Irish girl who taught the class was beautiful too—full of life. We had a little thing there for a while, but that's beside the point [laughter].

Maybe the thing I remember most was the May Day celebrations. Folks would get all dressed up in their finest clothes, which wasn't much in my case. There was a big parade of colonists waving the red flag. Then we had fun all day, played baseball, listened to poems, had a concert, and ate as good a feast as we could. It was really something. I was the shortstop for the ball team so I'd be in the game. I remember the catcher teasing me about my nickname, "Flash," because I had a bit of a hitch in my stride now after the injuries I got from the vigilantes in San Diego. "You don't look like no flash to me," he said. I was still fast enough to play though, and I got to a few tough balls up the middle and even ran out a double. If I wasn't "flash" anymore, I could sill get the job done sir [laughter].

We had an exhibition game that day, but other times we played other teams from around the valley. The Llano Sluggers, that was our name. I've always thought baseball was the best working-man's game. No clock to keep an eye on and outside in the fresh air. And anybody can play, fat or skinny, short or tall. You know that's where the idea for the first sit-downs came from don't you? A bunch a workers had sat down on the field to protest a bad call by an umpire in a ball league in Ohio and they thought, "Hey, this just might work on a factory floor too." But that's another story.

I remember one May Day afternoon sitting on a blanket in an almond grove with the teacher, Molly O'Conner was her name. There we were listening to folks reading poetry and then there was music with a beautiful mandolin and a saxophone. And the little ones were running 'round the Maypole. I remember I lied on my back and looked up at the big blue sky and everything seemed possible. Those were good days at Llano, real good days.

I looked over the notes in the back of the book and there was nothing about Bobby except a reference to the fact that he'd been in the I.W.W. and spent significant time at Llano. When the librarian announced that the place was closing, I asked her if she knew anything about the editor of the book, Joshua Cohen. All she could tell me was that he was an old leftist scholar who'd died a few years back. "Lots of these old comrades are passin' on," she said. I thanked her and asked if there was a place nearby where I could get a coffee. "Yum Yum Donuts," she said smiling impishly, "unless you want to drive all the way to USC for a Starbucks." I headed to my car and drove over to Yum Yum for a large coffee and a glazed donut. On the way in I got a "what are you doing around here, whiteboy?" look from a thoroughly tattooed guy on the corner. I tried to get a hold of Hank on the payphone outside by the liquor store down the block, but he didn't pick up. After that failure, I decided to find a cheap motel room in a little place I knew downtown on the edge of Chinatown. I took Normandie to Slauson and hit the 110 to downtown, got a room, and had Kung Pao Chicken and a Tsing Tao by myself in a lonely little restaurant across the street from a storefront Buddhist temple. So Bobby Flash had been a nickname, I mused—and a shortstop.

The next day, I got a hold of Hank and we decided to meet for lunch at PE Coles, the oldest bar in Los Angles and one of the competing homes of the French Dip Sandwich. I left my car at the motel and zig-zagged my way there, walking through Olvera Street and some folk musicians playing in the gazebo just outside the main shopping area, before crossing the street and meandering on past Union Station. In Little Tokyo, I looked at a coffee house where the Atomic Café had been and remembered from my reading that it was around here, at First and Los Angeles, where the Socialists had held their street meetings before they were banned. I wandered through an exhibit of art based on ecstatic states in the Geffen, leaving time to stop by the Bradbury Building on Broadway near Third. It was based on utopian socialist Edward Bellamy's esthetic principles, but had also been part of the dystopian future in *Blade Runner*. I'm not sure what I was hoping this would do for me, but I did wonder if Flash had ever walked these same streets. Here I turned the wrong way and ended up on Hill by Pershing Square where the Socialists moved their open air meetings after being banished from the streets. I got my bearings back and turned down 6th and walked toward skid row until I spotted the neon red sign on PE Cole's, "Since 1908."

Inside I looked for Hank, who wasn't there yet, even though my long aimless wander had made me fifteen minutes late. I ordered a Spaten dark at the bar and strolled around glancing at the black-and-white photos of Los Angeles that adorned the walls. There were shots of this area when it was the financial district, pictures of the old red cars and Los Angeles street life at the turn of the last century. I looked at the people on the street and imagined Bobby Flash or Blanco lost in these crowds, making their way to the Labor Temple or looking for a place to flop. I glanced down at a table top that had been the side of a Red Car before oil and tire money bought the trolley system out and shut them down leading to the empire of the automobile in Los Angeles. In the old days before the gentrification push began, this place had been a kind of an oasis from the rough streets, a good spot to kill time before catching the dog across the street at the Greyhound station. I remember the previous owner had a baseball bat ready at the first sign of trouble, like the time some guy tried to come in with a huge boa constrictor wrapped around his neck. I almost choked on my food when he yelled, "Get that fucking snake out of my bar, asshole!" It was a truly weird moment. Anyway, now somebody had bought Coles and, sadly, was "sprucing it up." At least they still had all the old pictures, for now.

I saw Hank come in and met him at the door with a hug. He smelled like cigarettes and he looked tired. He had dark circles around his green eyes. When he rubbed them he let his finger linger by the scar under his left eye—the one he got when he came to stay with me for a weekend as a young boy and ran into the corner of my end table. It took me years to live that one down. I noticed he seemed thinner. We each got French dips and sat at a booth by the bar to eat.

"What's up kid?" I asked.

"I just quit my job," he said with a half sheepish, half triumphant look about him. "I couldn't take my boss anymore. He was always on me about every little thing."

"What are you going to do now, take more classes?"

"With what money?"

"Aren't Trisha and Kurt supposed to be helping you? That's what they always tell me when I ask about you staying with me and going to school in San Diego."

"They're so far up their own assholes they don't even have time to think about it." He had a pained look and I stopped pushing. I'd learned long ago that my role as weekend hero only gave me limited authority.

"How about the Lakers?" I asked stupidly.

"I think Kurt is cheating on Mom," Hank said, ignoring my question. "He's never around and she's been really mopey. It's such a drag to be in that house, I'm telling you."

"Has she said anything to you?"

"No, I can just tell from the vibe they're giving off. It's like they have some kind of cold war going on that they are trying to keep between themselves, but it's obvious what's going on."

"That's quite a metaphor," I said unable to stop smiling.

"Fuck off, Dad," he said laughing a bit. "The Lakers are the Kobe show as usual. As long as he's healthy, they'll be alright."

"Good supporting cast though."

"I wouldn't want to see an injury. Kobe gets hurt, they're done."

"You know," I broke in, "you could think about moving to San Diego if the situation at home is so bad it gets in the way."

"Is that all you ever think about, my finishing school? It's not like a degree is going to guarantee me anything better than you've been able to do." I looked at him tenderly as he rubbed his mustard-stained hands on his napkin. His thick, shaggy, brown hair was uncombed and he had on a plain black t-shirt that half-covered the skull and crossbones he'd had tattooed on his left shoulder. It said "*carpe diem*" under it. This was always where the conversation ended, with his idealized version of my dead end career as a "journalist."

"You're smarter than me. You could do better," I said trying to make light of the situation while still driving the point home.

"Bullshit," he said with finality. I gave up, and when he asked me what I was doing, I told him about Bobby Flash. He was pretty fired up about it. He'd read a little bit about the Wobblies in a history class and thought they sounded cool. He had also been intrigued when I passed on the family legend about our leftist progenitor. It was then that I thought it might be fun to take him to Llano.

We paid for our lunch and grabbed a cab back to the motel parking lot where my car was. It was still early afternoon and we had plenty of time to get out to the Antelope Valley before rush hour locked up the grid. We took the 10 East to the 15 North through the smog-brown heart of the Inland Empire. On the way to the turnoff for the Pearblossom Highway, I told Hank about the roots of the old colony and mentioned that Aldous Huxley had lived out in Llano and that the highway had been the subject of a pretty cool collage by David Hockney. Just as I was about to say something about Huxley and his LA days, Hank took out his iPod and plugged me in as I drove toward the exurbs on the western tip of the Mojave Desert. It was a song by Frank Black, of Pixies fame, called "Rio del Llano." I smiled and listened to Frank sing about looking for utopia "in the stucco grids and the tumbleweeds." There was even a line about looking for Huxley

"between the power lines and the purple flowers of mescaline."
I unplugged myself and asked him why he didn't tell me that he
knew about Llano earlier. He just smiled at me with a rare aura
of superiority.

"The wind tastes like gasoline out here," he said paraphras-
ing the song. We drove out into the desert through Pinion Hills
until we found Llano. I pulled off the highway and we walked
out to the ruins, gazing up at what remained of the old hotel's
stone arroyo walls and columns. We saw a big round building
with square holes that may have been windows or something else.
Hank strolled around silently inspecting the stones. He looked
strangely moved by the whole thing. I looked over across the desert toward the mountains in the distance and tried to imagine
Bobby Flash hauling these stones. Where had the ball field been?
The orchards? The almond grove where he listened to music with
Molly O'Conner? It was probably just my imagination, but I felt
a sense of presence somehow. Hank kicked an empty Coke bottle
and it flew up in the air and bounced off an abandoned tire sitting
amidst the scrub brush and creosote. Lots of the locals seemed
to have found utopia a suitable spot for a garbage dump. I was
surprised by how much traffic there had been on the highway in
what used to be the sticks. Now it was just another place to com-
mute from.

Hank had climbed up on a wall and was sitting down, staring toward the horizon, at nothing in particular. I climbed up
next to him and put my arm around him. He let me. If I could
have thought of a way to express my absolute wonder at the fact
that my baby boy was now a man I would have, but everything
that came to mind seemed utterly trite. He was the only gift I'd
given to the world that was full of hope. I thought of trying to
say something about how everything would work out fine, how

his Mom would survive even if Kurt left for good, but I didn't. We just sat there, side by side, as the afternoon surrendered to twilight, mingling with unnamed ghosts and pondering the ruins of the perfect future.

8

When I got back into San Diego after my week off, I checked into the office and Neville was uncharacteristically friendly. He asked about my son and told me he hoped I'd gotten some rest. Something about his effusive welcome and sudden concern about my family life gave me pause, but I didn't push it.

Unfortunately, the freelance photographer I was supposed to take with me to my follow up visit to Tijuana had the flu. I had to go that day and I only had one back up, my old girlfriend Samantha. Sam and I had broken up badly. Perhaps it would be more accurate to say that she'd dumped me like a hot potato for a guitar player, ten years her junior. He was the lead guitar player for the Crystal Meth Trailer Park, a local band that was the next big thing. She'd gone out to take a few shots for our music writer, who was doing a review, and ended up going home with the guy that night. We were done by the end of the week and she acted like it was no big deal. Well, I'm not the jealous type, but I was amused that the review turned out to be a pretty bad one, "Trailer trash disappoints." It ended up that the guitar player disappointed too, dumping Samantha, while on tour, for a younger model. He just showed up at their next local show with the new one and cut Sam cold. Instant Karma, I thought.

In any event, I called Sam and got her right away. She was not particularly enthused at the idea of working with me.

"Are you kidding?" she asked when I pitched the gig.

"Nope, I need you bad," I said, enjoying her discomfort.

She agreed hesitantly and we made plans to meet in San Ysidro by the trolley stop.

"How's the rock star?" I inquired, with a shit-eating grin.

"Just shut the fuck up and be a professional about this," she said as if that meant anything to me.

"Just curious how you're doing," I said with as much feigned innocence as I could muster. "Is that a crime?"

"You know what happened," she said. "Maybe I should just get back on the trolley and head home if you're going to be an asshole."

"No, no. Please stay, I'm sorry," I said, still smiling. "What the fuck were you thinking?"

"Can we not talk about this?" she asked, pleadingly.

"OK," I said after a long pause, "let's go meet Ricardo." As we made our way through the border maze, Sam walked in front of me and I watched her purposeful, yet graceful stride, and admired the way her long red hair was arranged underneath a bandana. She was in her late thirties but could easily pass for late twenties with her rosy-cheeked exuberance. Only a certain elegance of carriage revealed her age. I felt bad that I had been so tough on her. After all, it must have been humiliating for her to get thrown over by some kid. *She* was supposed to be the one tossing men aside. It was probably a stark reminder that time was not on her side, not on anyone's side. I followed her through the clanging metal turnstiles to where Ricardo greeted us warmly. I introduced Samantha and we walked over to Ricardo's Jeep for our tour.

Before we got to the neighborhood where the Madres Unidas lived, Ricardo asked us if we'd like to see the industrial part of the city. We agreed, and he drove us to a street lined with several large maquiladoras. The first one was a place were they made television components. We parked across the street and walked over to a lunch truck where Ricardo lingered to see if the security guards were up front. They weren't, so he took us stealthily around a corner where we looked inside a window at rows of workers packed into the warehouse. When a door opened, you could smell the pungent fumes pouring out. Sam snapped a few shots, and Ricardo motioned for us to follow him and pointed out a huge metal tube that was pouring what, at first glance, appeared to be water down a hillside that led to a neighborhood below.

"Toxic," he said. "And where does it go? Right into the streets down there." A pair of large men rounded the corner behind us and Ricardo didn't need to tell us to run as we read the menace in their expressions. We got to the Jeep with about twenty-five yards to spare, and Ricardo took off at full speed with the men running behind us for about half a block.

"They would have taken your camera," he said calmly, "and kicked my ass." We drove about a mile and stopped outside another factory where one shift of workers was leaving, to be replaced at once by another. I thought of a scene in the silent film *Metropolis* where the workers walk in rows into the door of a factory that has been transformed into the gaping maw of a monster. A group of workers recognized Ricardo and walked over to shake his hand. They looked behind them as they spoke. Another set of security guards started to walk across the street and Ricardo took off at once.

"Those men both have cancer," he said. "Everyone who works there long enough gets sick in one way or another. The company just hires new workers when the old ones get too sick. They deny any connection between the chemicals in the plant and the illnesses. And the workers are too powerless to do anything."

"What do they make in there?" Sam asked.

"That's where your batteries come from," he said pointing to her camera. She looked down, took a shot of the row of factories behind us. We passed a place that made dolls, a place that produced IV tubes, a place that made lenses for glasses where the workers went blind from their labors. Finally, we stopped at the site of the old battery factory and walked over to the top of the hill where the waste was buried. Down below us was the neighborhood where Las Madres lived. Sam took a good number of shots of rusty barrels and a fading warning sign complete with a skull and cross bones. She took a few more shots of the neighborhood below.

"When it rains," Ricardo told her, "the waste pours down the hill to where their children play." We walked back to the Jeep and drove down a winding dirt road to meet the women. A group of them were there with a plate of tamales to share with us. I could tell that Samantha was touched by the gesture. I watched her eat one carefully and compliment the cook before she got to work. I shook hands with the women I remembered from my first visit. They were all there but Marisol, the older woman.

"*Donde esta Marisol?*" I managed in my bad Spanish.

"She is at the doctor with one of her grandchildren," Ricardo said after Rosa whispered something in his ear. I got a few more quotes for my piece and walked down the street with Sam as she worked silently, but efficiently, taking pictures of houses made out of discarded garage doors, children playing soccer next to puddles of toxic waste, women cooking over makeshift stoves for their families after twelve-hour shifts in the maquilas. Sam walked over to a group of children and got them to pose for a picture, and I took the time to ask Ricardo if the security was unusual today.

"It was nothing," he said. "I've been arrested many times, beaten up, threatened with guns. The police are on the side of the maquiladora owners, so are the politicians." I nodded and noticed that Samantha had stopped and was checking her bag. She found her last memory card and went over to take portraits of the women. A man in one of the houses offered us beers. I said thanks but no, as did Ricardo. He was looking up at the dirt road where a van was heading down the hill fast. It was a group of men from one of the maquiladoras. They screeched to a halt and bounded out of the van demanding Samantha's camera from Ricardo. He said no and a big man in a cowboy hat and dark glasses got up in his face and screamed something I couldn't understand. Then he struck Ricardo on the face with his hand, hard enough to knock him to his knees. As he got to his feet, I noticed that a group of men from the neighborhood had come out of their houses with bats and pieces of wood. Behind them, some of the women had pans or garden tools. The crowd grew slowly with more people coming to join them. The man who had hit Ricardo looked over at Samantha with her camera alongside a group of women standing in front of Rosa's house. He said, "Be careful with that, bitch" in English, and motioned to the other men to get back into the van. They sped off, and Ricardo took off down a different road with us and a group of men in a neighbor's pick-up truck. "Print the pictures on the front page," he said as we drove off hastily.

The guy driving the pick up took a long circuitous route that got us to the border without further incident. Along the way, we got a tour of the poorest barrios in the city, gazing out the back of the truck at shack after shack full of people not lucky enough to even have a crappy job in the maquilas. I was covered with dust by the time we got to a paved road, and Sam was staring out of the side of the truck silently, deep in thought. The men dropped us at the line, slapped us on the back, and drove back to the dust and menace. Standing in line at the border, I apologized to Sam for getting her in the middle of a fix.

"Don't apologize," she said. "It was incredible, those women, the courage of those people."

I told her I agreed and thought she'd done an amazing job. She wiped some dirt of the side of my face and kissed me on the cheek. We crossed the border and were greeted by a crowd of men waving American flags and signs that said, "Keep America American." It was the New Patriot Militia, the same group I'd covered when they started patrolling the border a few years ago. At the time, they'd gone from driving down en masse and aiming their high beams across the border to setting up extralegal checkpoints manned by armed "patriots." They had an official website that shied away from controversy but anybody who'd ever been out there with them had heard the racial slurs and threats.

When the counter-protesters showed up, things got ugly, and someone across the line ended up getting shot, but they lived and nobody was ever charged. I'll always remember one day when the militia caught a migrant woman with a small child and tried to detain them for the border patrol, and the counter-protesters, a mixture of kids in local MEChA groups and immigrants rights advocates from around the region, started pulling her away, with the kid in the middle. The chant of "Let them go!" broke out, followed by a general melee. The woman and her kid got away but there were some bloodied activists afterwards. By the time the border patrol got there, it was he said/she said, but they started separating the groups after that. It was only a matter of time until one of those fuckers in the militia was going to kill someone.

After today, I was in no mood to be screwed with by vigilantes. One of the patriots tried to pass me a flyer and I told him to go fuck himself. He shoved me and I knocked the sign out of his hand. I looked him straight in the eyes with my best, "don't fuck with me" look, but he sneered at me and started to go for something in his pocket. Just as he was reaching and I was raising a fist, a cop came over and broke us up. Good thing too, because I could have killed the asshole. Samantha had gotten a shot of the guy pushing me before the cop got there. The cop told her to put the camera away and she took his picture instead. He put up his hand and I got in between them.

"We're going," I said, grabbing her around the waist and walking her toward the trolley.

"I can't fucking believe them," she said.

"It's been a long day," I replied. She calmed down and told me she'd driven and could give me a ride back to my place if I wanted. Heading up I-5, we debriefed about the day and figured out our timeline for the story. She said she'd get right on the pictures that night. When she parked on the street by my studio, I leaned over to give her a kiss. She put her hand on my leg and looked at me tenderly.

"I think we're better off being friends," she told me. I got out of the car and watched her drive away, wondering what had gotten into me.

The next day, Samantha emailed me a batch of fantastic photos and I finished the article on Las Madres Unidas by the end of the week, adding in our adventures with the vigilantes on both sides of the border. Neville loved it and slated it for the cover of the next week's edition. He picked a picture Samantha had gotten of Ricardo being shoved by the security guy and entitled the piece, "The High Costs of Cheap Labor." I was really proud of this one and would have been content to rest on my laurels over the weekend if I hadn't gotten a call back from the People's Archive up in San Francisco. I'd left a message on their answering machine asking if they had any material on the Wobblies in San Diego, Bobby Flash in particular. Yes on both counts was the answer, so I got out my credit card and got a ticket on an airbus to San Francisco.

I got there early on Friday and my appointment at the People's Archive was on Saturday, so I had the whole day to play with. It was a crisp, but clear February morning and I was happy to be in the city. I took the BART to the Muni from the airport and got off the N Judah near UCSF. From there, I walked over to Kezar Stadium to meet Shane who'd come down from his new digs up on the Lost Coast. He was sitting on the steps down by the running track watching the joggers when I found him.

"Hey, what are you doing in the big bad city, man?" I said as I hugged him.

"I'm lost," he said, smiling.

"How are things in the cult?" I goaded him.

"Fuck off," he said. "Is that what you think I'm doing?"

"Just kidding," I replied. "To be honest, I have no idea what you're doing."

Shane leaned back and stretched. "Let's go for a walk," he said. "You ever been to Sutro Baths?" I told him I hadn't but I was game and we started on our way. Shane looked great, healthy and happy. He seemed different somehow, less restless. We crossed the street and headed into Golden Gate Park where we wandered toward the sea going on side trips through the arboretum and around Stow Lake. As always, I enjoyed taking in the lush green of the park that stood in stark contrast to San Diego's desert dry. Shane and I marveled at how both the '49ers and the Raiders used to play at Kezar. I told him about a Hunter S. Thompson piece I read on the subject, which portrayed the Niners fans as mean drunken louts. We laughed and kept on trucking past the Polo Fields and the Buffalo Paddock. I stopped for a second and watched some kids practicing at the fly-casting pools. Finally, we got to the end of the park and Shane suggested we grab a drink at a nice restaurant next to the Dutch windmill. We sat down at a table on the outside patio area. I got a beer and Shane ordered a sparkling water.

"Water, huh?" I said a little taken aback at his newly found moderation. "Are you sure you haven't joined a cult?"

"We've got a bit more to walk," he replied refusing to take the bait. "I'm pacing myself." I laughed and let it rest, choosing instead to enjoy my beer and his company. It was one of those sublimely gorgeous San Francisco days and everything looked ethereal in the winter sunlight. I could hear the surf just across the road and a seagull landed on a pine tree branch above us.

"You should come up and visit me at the collective," Shane said. "We have big parties and people come from all over the place. It's a great time. Everybody brings a different kind of food, usually food they've grown themselves. People stay overnight for a couple days sometimes. It's kind of a community tradition. I can let you know the next time something is coming up." I looked at him and he seemed totally earnest, devoid of any hint of irony. It worried me, but I just sat there and listened. It turned out he was part of a collective that shared the profits from various enterprises—farming, fishing, crafts, and a host of other things. He was working with some people who had invited him to help do conservation work for the river estuary. There was a woman who had an idea for sustainable ecotourism that could bring in lots of money. And a retired teacher wanted to start a camp for poor kids from places like Oakland who'd never been out of the city. They could come up in the summer, stay at the collective, go on hikes in the woods, and learn about ecology. This retired teacher he'd met had actually done some research on kids who'd never had any access to the wild and she'd discovered that some urban problems might actually be attributable to what she called "a nature deficit disorder." I was intrigued. It sounded less flaky than I had initially suspected.

We finished our drinks and crossed the street and walked for a ways until we hit the remains of Sutro Baths, a decadent public bathhouse that had thrived earlier in the twentieth century. Now all that was left were the ruins of the buildings. We climbed around them and took a path that led to a spot where you could see the Golden Gate Bridge spanning the sparkling Bay. I was panting a bit, and Shane put his hand on my shoulder.

"You're not getting enough exercise, are you?" he smirked. Then he got serious, took a breath and said, "You know, you don't need to worry about me. I know what I'm doing. For once in my life, I feel like I'm actually building something durable. It's not just tilting at windmills." Clearly, he had read the suspicion on my face.

"I believe you," I said, feeling a little bad about my knee-jerk reaction to his new life. "It's just not something I ever thought about before."

"It's off the grid," he said smiling.

"Yeah," I said, "I guess it is."

On Saturday I got to the People's Archive for my appointment in the late morning. It was located on the second floor of a big loft building in the Mission. I had to call up to get buzzed in and was met at the top of the stairs by Pete, an amiable old fellow with a handlebar moustache. He was wearing an ILWU hat. After we shook hands, he walked me over to the main desk and handed me a stack of things related to my request.

"I think you're going to be happy with these," he said. I took the stack and went over to sit on an ancient ratty couch next to a scuffed coffee table that served as their reading room. Pete left me to my business and got back to listening to Ornette Coleman and reading a mystery novel behind the desk. I settled in and started looking over the material. The first few things were amazing—original issues of *Solidarity* and *Industrial Worker* covering the San Diego free speech fight. I read over accounts of the struggle and skimmed through the fragile old pages, looking at the Mr. Block cartoons and admiring the artistic sketches depicting fat bosses in top hats and heroic workers marching into the new dawn. As fascinating as these were, there was no reference to Bobby Flash or Gus Blanco. It was frustrating because they had enough papers to cover the events of that period episodically, but not the entire run of issues. Still it was more than I had seen in one place anywhere else.

After I was done looking through the Wobbly papers, I leafed through an original copy of the anarchist publication *Mother Earth* with an account of the San Diego affair. There was a lot on Goldman there, still nothing on Flash. Under the copy of *Mother Earth*, they even had a few I.W.W. posters and some postcards from the Magónista revolt in Tijuana and a poster of "The Pyramid of the Capitalist System." I was just about to go over and ask about Bobby Flash when I came upon the second to last item, a comb-bound typed manuscript from the early sixties. It was entitled, *Black Cat Days: Conversations with Western Wobblies*. The word "DRAFT" was stamped on the front cover as well as on the title page. I flipped it open to the table of contents and saw that the manuscript was a collection of interviews with former Wobblies, one of whom was Bobby Flash. I raced to his interview and read:

> In my Wobbly days, I went by Bobby Flash or Buckshot Jack, but Bobby Flash mostly. I had a couple of other aliases I used once or twice in a pinch, but Flash seemed to stick. I got the name as a kid playing baseball because I was quick to the ball. My born name was Jack Wilson.

Jack Wilson! I stopped, put down the book and said "no" out loud. When I picked the manuscript back up and reread the words, it was still there, "Jack Wilson." The coincidence was too weird to be true, I thought. I read on:

My mother was a fine woman, a schoolteacher in my home-town of Eureka. She taught me how to read as a boy and cared for my brother and me even as my father was bent on drinking himself to death. Mother died of cancer when I was just 15 and things got real bad. My father owned a little general store in town. My brother Frank and me used to work in the store for Pop and when Mom died he started drinking harder and beating us for every little thing. As things went down hill with his business, he took it out on us. Frank was the first to leave about a year after mother died. He took off on a freight car and we never heard from him again. I stuck it out for another year or two, but Dad got dead drunk when he lost the busi-ness, and I decided that I wasn't about to take another beating so I laid him out with a two by four and he went down hard. I didn't wait to see if he woke up or not, but I heard later that he survived it. Anyway, I hit the rails like Frank and spent a good amount of time lookin' for him, though I'm sad to say I never heard a word about him anywhere for the rest of my life. My pop died a year or two after I took off, so by the time I was twenty I was pretty much on my own.

Life on the rails seemed like a big adventure at first. I was happy to be out from under Pop's thumb and I'd never been anywhere in my life. Back in town, I'd heard stories from some of the timberbeasts that all a man had to do was hop a freight and there was work to be had just about anywhere. Pop had treated us boys like dogs so the idea of hard work didn't scare me. And, I thought, this way the money I earned would stay in my own pocket, not go straight for Pop's whiskey. So I can remember sitting on an open car as it went along, staring up at the redwoods with the sun shining down through the trees thinking I had it made. Pretty soon, I learned that those timberbeast tales were a little sugar coated. The sidecars got cold as hell at night and old dirty face (that's what we called the trains) was a hard place to sleep. Plus, the rattlers (that's the cars) was full of hijacks who could spot a dumb kid real easy. Well, I got robbed and beat up on my first night and I only avoided greasing the wheels when some other fellas chased off the hijack. "Greasing the wheels" was when a boy got thrown down under the train and mashed to death by the wheels. I saw it happen a time or two and it made me wise real quick.

The fellow that saved me was a good sort and once he heard my story he sort of showed me the ropes. I learned who to look out for and who to trust. Back in the days before the Wobs it was a nasty business riding the rails. The hijacks or the cops or the railroad company thugs was always after you. Well, this fellow also warned me about the labor sharks who'd play up the work in every town and then you'd show up and find out it wasn't all peaches and cream like he said it was. So, with that rough initiation, I became a bindlestiff or a blanket stiff or a harvest stiff. Whatever you want to call it. Those were all the names they had for the migratory worker. Later folks started to call us hobos, but we were stiffs first.

My first job off the train was as a harvest stiff, helping with a grain harvest up in Oregon. I just about broke my back working the first day and this fellow comes up to me and says, "Look kid, they ain't gonna pay you a dime more for killing yourself, so why don't you give us all a break and slow down?" I saw his point when I got my first check. The food we got was rot too and no bunks or decent blankets in the camps either. I remember boiling clothes in a pot of water the first time to get them clean after some fellow taught me that. I couldn't believe they'd treat men like this. From there on I did a little of whatever I could get. I worked as a timberbeast; I worked in the fields; I washed dishes; I hauled rocks at construction sites; I loaded ships on the waterfront; I worked on a boat or two; I worked on a ranch; I picked just about anything that can grow on a tree; I saw the worst a man can do to another man.

After about two years of ramblin' about I had seen just about enough of workingmen getting their teeth kicked in time after time. There was a camp I was in where they nailed the men's plates to the tables so they wouldn't be stolen and hosed 'em down after we ate, like we were animals in a barnyard. I saw men worked to death, literally. A fellow dropped dead next to me on a construction site out in the desert one time and they just dragged him off and hollered at us to keep working. Not a single word spent or a minute of silence. They just plopped another stiff in his place and kept the machine going. That's how it was. We were no better than parts, expendable human parts in the capitalist system. Surplus labor the Marxists would call us. It was dog eat dog out there.

After a while, I got pretty damn hard. There was a point when I would have just as soon killed a boss or thug or some other respectable citizen as look at 'em. In the camps there was a whole different world, the jungle we used to call it. Well, in the jungle there were a whole lot of honest hardworking stiffs and there were some criminals too. Sometimes, I admit that I'd hear some boys talking and laughing about robbing some fat cat and I started to think it wasn't such a bad idea. Why the hell should some lazy son of a bitch sit around and count the money he made off our backs? Now, later I came to realize that a lot of them fellas was just gamblers and con artists who'd just as soon rob another worker as a fat cat, but the anger was settling into me and I can be sure that I would have murdered some son of bitch if it hadn't of been for the I.W.W.

As it was, I got pretty good at defending myself. I carried a razor and an old spike in case I got in a scrape and word got around that I was no longer easy pickings. Plus, I was quick too if the situation was not in my favor. I first got tagged with "Flash" as a kid playing ball, but later some fellow called me Flash after he saw me catch a freight that was pulling away real fast. The boys on the trains yelled for me to stop but I made the jump anyway and was on in a flash. So the name stuck. I started using Bobby after I got arrested for vagrancy in Washington and was dumb enough to give my real name. That's how Bobby Flash was born. It was my name as a bindlestiff, riding the rails. And I came to prefer it. It was the name I earned on my own. And the man that nicknamed me was a Wob too. I didn't know it at first but later he caught a hijack trying to shake down a little fellow who was an easy mark. Well, this fellow, Reno Sam, nails the hijack from behind and cuts I.W.W. on his forehead, real deep, so everyone would know where he got his comeuppance. Pretty soon, we stopped seeing hijacks on that line.

Well that was about 1909. After I met Reno Sam we went together to a job on a farm in Northern California and he organized a strike to get us a few cents more per bushel. The farmer didn't have a choice since his crop had to be picked soon or it would have rotted. So we got a better share. I had never even heard of a union, so Reno Sam's little maneuver was the most amazing thing I'd ever seen. For once, we didn't get our teeth kicked in. Pretty soon after, Reno told me all about the One Big Union while were riding the rails. It wasn't anything theoretical at all. It was, "Why shouldn't the folks who do all the work get a better deal? Why should the hard workers get slop while the boss is eating pork chops? You ever see a fat man on the rails? Why can't all the workers get together for their fair share?" It was belly philosophy. You get the picture. After that, I joined the I.W.W. and got my card, which I still have to this day.

Once I was part of the One Big Union, a door opened to a whole other world. The Wobblies used to say that they turned "bums into men" and, in my case, it was true. For me, the I.W.W. represented having dignity. It was about being a human being not an animal. That's what the Wobblies were about. We were the knights of the road and we were through being pushed around. As a Wobbly, you pushed back and you pushed the right fellows. It wasn't like my father who beat us boys because he couldn't fight the folks who pushed him out of business or the criminals who took their revenge on whoever they could. We were there to go after the bosses and, eventually, end their game completely. Slowly, I got to understanding a bit more about the whole philosophy, but I was a Western Wob and Western Wobs was not the real philosophical types. There were different camps. Lots of the city Wobs from the east coast could talk your ear off, but they couldn't do shit. Out west, the migratory workers dominated the organization and we were more inclined to direct action without much debate.

Still, around the fires in the jungles, we'd get to debating all kinds of things. Some of the organizers were real hard on drinking and talked about how the saloons robbed workers of pay and brought them to ruin. This was agreed to by some, but met with derision by others who say the other Wobs "sounded like the god damned Salvation Army." That got a big laugh and we'd get along all right despite disagreements on this issue or that. Another topic that split folks was nonviolence. Some of the Wobs was for strict nonviolence as the use of violence only gave the cops and the bosses an excuse. I remember one fellow, "the Priest" we used to call him on account of his high principles, was very passionate about this question. He'd talk about violence being a product of capitalism and how we should have no use for it as we'd mostly just be using it against fellow workers, etc., etc. Some of the other boys would say that

that sounded mighty good, but it was hard to practice when you were getting your head busted in. That would get laughs too. Still, as a tactic, I came to understand what they were talking about. And it did work too, sometimes. That same fellow, Giovanni was his real name, ended up dead after being forced to run a gauntlet out in San Diego. Ultimately, I came to see the violence on the other side as so huge, that it was just too much to ask a man to be a saint all the time. We had about as much chance as a rabbit before a gunner sometimes. It made you mad as hell. So we got our shots in too, when the time was right.

Later on in the organization, that same split between the bindlestiffs and city folks (although it was more sloppy than that really) came up again when the communists won over in Russia. Lots of the Wobs who were sympathetic to the revolution in Russia thought that we were too undisciplined. They thought we needed a tighter organization. So they moved toward the CP, while a lot of the old Wobs bucked up against the hard CP line. The CP types didn't always have the best sense of humor and lots of Wobs didn't trust a man who couldn't laugh at himself. That and they didn't like the idea of *anybody* telling them what to do, even other radicals. We were an untamed bunch, we were. I came to side with the anarchists who didn't trust the CP in the end. What did Emma Goldman say, "If I can't dance, I don't want to be part of your revolution"? Something like that. Well, despite all these kinds of arguments, we mostly got along. When it came to a struggle, theory didn't matter that much. It was simply "which side are you on," and we would die for each other. I know it sounds farfetched, but it was true.

I remember getting hooked up with a great organizer, Gus Blanco, out in Holtville. I had been working as a dishwasher out there and Gus called a meeting and let us know that there was a revolution in the works in Mexico. So Gus and I were part of that. We were in the first raid that took Mexicali, and we were in both battles of Tijuana. It was a hell of a time down there too. For a while, I really believed we had something started. The red flag was flying over the center of Tijuana and we had folks flooding into town to see the Wobbly army.

I stopped here and went through my folder and reread the interview I'd found about the Magónista revolt. The account in the manuscript matched the other interview closely, nearly word for word in places. I was on to something it seemed. I kept skimming through this portion until I found a new wrinkle:

> We lost some fine comrades down there, but I had a good time too. There was a fellow named Dynamite Dan who managed to sneak off with a couple good bottles of tequila before Pryce could bust 'em all up. Well, Dan and I holed up and had a drink in this little shack, and while we were there, I caught sight of a beautiful girl hanging some laundry. I couldn't get her out of my head, and the next day I came around to see if she was there and we wound up going for a walk. It turned out she was in sympathy with the revolution and we did the best job we could of talking between English and Spanish. At the end of the day, we became lovers, and I think I would have married her if we hadn't been run out of town after the second battle. Later, I heard from some of the boys who'd been back down there that she'd given birth to a child that was half gringo. Was it my child? I never found out.

Here the narrative stopped. It was missing a few pages too. Damn it, I thought, what a piece to leave hanging. The next page picked up after a heading, "Soapboxing Days":

The first time I got up on a soapbox, I would have just as soon have run a gauntlet. My stomach was tied in knots and I could hear some fellows laughing at the pained expression that must have been on my face. But then some jackass yelled, "Get that bum off the box" and I got mad. That was all it took, "Yeah, bums, that's what they call us," I started in. "You can smell 'em before you see 'em is what they say. They say the fine ladies should be protected against seeing shabby fellas like us." Well, somebody said, "You tell 'em brother" and that was all I needed. I got going about the bosses eatin' good while we were starving and all that stuff. As I said, it was the belly philosophy that really hit people.

When a good street meeting really got going it was like a carnival. Other folks would speak too, the Salvation Army and the like, but nobody could match us Wobs on the soapbox. We used to make fun of the preachers and some of them would get so worked up they'd stomp off and call a cop. Sometimes we'd go back and forth with socialists about voting versus the general strike too. But the thing that really stood out was ordinary folks getting a chance to speak their minds. We were mostly interested in organizing, but I can see now how important we were in the struggle for freedom for ordinary folks. We forced America's hand. You say you have free speech, we'll give it to you. They didn't like it of course. We scared the hell out of the bosses and they got dangerous when they were scared. They killed men to shut them up. Think about that, killing a man to stop him from speaking. What kind of freedom is that?

I seen the worst of it in San Diego where I got to run the gauntlet, and I seen the worst of it again in Minot, North Dakota where the vigilantes came after us again. It was a bloody business, those fights. My buddy Blanco got murdered up in Everett in 1916. Never had a chance against them vigilantes up there.

I stopped and checked the date against my notes. Blanco had wondered aloud about Flash's fate in his narrative about the San Diego fight, but it turns out that it was Gus, not Bobby who failed to escape the vigilantes' wrath. He'd survived the Denver fight, but not the struggle to speak in Everett. I looked over at Pete who was still lost in his mystery even after his jazz CD had stopped. The next section of the manuscript was called, "In the Pen." I read on:

> During the free speech fights it was our strategy to fill the jails. The cops would pull in a dozen of us and we'd send a hundred more. At first it drove the police to their wits' end. In San Diego we had so many folks in the jails they couldn't take any more. That's what led them to up the ante and resort to vigilante justice in my opinion. They just couldn't tame us in jail. I remember hearing a story at one of the hobo colleges once about how when Ralph Waldo Emerson came to visit Henry David Thoreau, who was in jail for not paying his taxes to protest the Mexican war, he asked him, "What are you doing in there?" And Henry's response was, "What are you doing out there?" Well, that was our attitude. If there was a struggle involving fellow Wobs it was a badge of honor to go to jail.

> We'd start giving 'em hell right from the start. They'd ask for our name and we'd say "Joe Hill" or something like that and they'd get riled up and then we'd give them some other made-up name. They'd ask for our family and we'd say, "none." They'd ask for our best friend and we'd say "Big Bill Haywood" or something like that. When they got to asking for our home address, we'd always say it was the jail we were in at the time or say "a side car" or just give 'em the last place we'd been.

> When there was a bunch of us in there, we'd run our affairs and make our decisions by a committee system and we'd come

up with ways to frustrate the jailors. We'd have a hunger strike to try to get better food than the dry bread or pig intestines they'd toss in the pen. If they was beating us badly, we'd raise hell until they couldn't take it any more. In San Diego and Fresno and Denver and all over the place, the jailors hated the singing. We'd go into "Solidarity" or "Hold the Fort" or "Hallelujah, I'm a Bum" or some other song and keep it going for hours so they could hardly think straight. In lots of places, they'd send in the Bible thumpers to save our souls on Sunday and they'd start singing to us and we'd steal the tunes but change the words so the songs made sense. There weren't hardly any religious Wobs that I ever knew. We all saw it for the scam it was, just another way to keep the working man down. Down and obedient. But they sure didn't like being made fun of, I'll tell you that. It was real trying on their Christian charity.

It was a joke to send in the preachers when they were treating us like animals. We'd get the "steam cleaning" in some of the jails, which meant getting blasted off with hot water. Other jails, they used cold water. We never had enough bunks either, so most of us would sleep on the floor on a dirty blanket or sometimes nothing at all on cold steel. In San Diego, the conditions got so bad at one point that they had to release a whole load of Wobs to avoid an epidemic after a Wob came down with small pox I think it was. If they were being real cruel, then we'd build a battleship. That was when all the boys in a cell would join arms and jump together. If there were enough of us in the pen, the battleship would shake the jail to the foundations. If we were upstairs, it would put the fear into them that the floor was gonna collapse. It was a hell of a way to get their attention, that's for sure.

I don't mean to suggest that it was just a big party in there though. Despite the solidarity of the boys, some of the men would get discouraged from being kicked around so much and lots of fellows got real sick. After a long jail stay, sometimes it'd take a good while to get your health back. You had to heal your wounds and eat proper for a few weeks after the horrible garbage they threw us in the pen. I lost some teeth from my jail time and got a few aches that have never gone away. That was the price you paid, though, it was the price you paid for standing up like a man. It was be a slave or fight, and we chose to fight.

There were a few more pages missing and what looked to be some notes by the editor about following up with more questions. "Which jails during which struggles?" read one note. "Ask about Fresno" read another. The next typed entry was "Hobo Colleges and Communes":

One thing you don't hear much about anymore was the fact that there was a Hobo College or a Colony or Commune of some type in or on the outskirts of almost every city. They weren't all run by Wobblies, but Wobs were there. They were run by sympathetic folks, "fellow travelers" the communists used to call them later, I think. Sometimes it would just be a red boarding house that everybody coming off the road would stay in once they found out about them. Then there were bars and coffee houses too that everyone knew to go to when you were looking for like-minded folks. The most famous hobo college was Ben Reitman's in Chicago. I saw Emma Goldman speak there and she was terrific. Very passionate, but not too practical. Still I loved to sit and listen to folks talk about politics or literature or just about anything else you could think of to talk about. I stopped at a colony set up by Wobs and Socialists in the hills in Arkansas where they had a real school. I saw a debate about voting versus direct action at a red hall in New Orleans.

There was a camp by the tracks in Seattle run by a bunch of folks who believed in Free Love. They were anarchists, I believe. The idea was that nobody owned anybody and that women would only be free and equal when marriage was ended. This seemed like an invitation to an orgy to some of the boys as there just weren't a whole lot of women on the rails in those days, but they were pretty quickly taught the error of their ways by some of the women. To be in with that crowd, any woman had to be high spirited and tough. And there were a good number of them. I have to say that on the road, sometimes the only women you'd have contact with were prostitutes. I knew a good number of gals who made their living that way in the camps. It was a hard life though and many came to bad ends. It seemed to me that it was the most degraded aspect of capitalism that love was for sale. Still is, even in the way folks marry into money and such. That's just a respectable form of prostitution if you ask me, but that's another story.

Some of my favorite lectures in the Hobo Colleges were on Walt Whitman. I heard this one fellow give a talk about what Whitman's view of the world was—what it could be like after a revolution, when folks could live their lives fully, like human beings and not as slaves to a clock. He spoke a lot too about the way Whitman saw the human body as holy, and sex as holy, and nature as holy, and how every man had the answer to life's puzzle in themselves. I wasn't ever religious in any way, but perhaps if I was, Whitman's idea of what's holy lined up well with what matters most to me.

So there were a lot of talks on things like that. Folks would talk about Oscar Wilde, Karl Marx, Edward Bellamy. And it's funny that a lot of men that looked all scruffy, and that respectable folks would shy away from, would be sitting in these Hobo Colleges hungry for ideas. That's the thing, folks still talk about workers like a bunch of dumb stiffs, but a lot of the boys, even with no formal education to speak of, had more to them than people think. There were some real smart folks that could have been lawyers or professors or something like that if they hadn't been born into the working class. So they put all their energy into the One Big Union. It was our university, our church, our philosophy of life.

Maybe the best experience I had with schools was at the Llano Colony. Llano del Rio Colony they called it, down in the desert by Los Angeles. It was there I met Miss Molly O'Conner who was a schoolteacher, socialist, and believer in Free Love. I fell in love with her during my first stay at the Llano Colony when I went to a lecture she gave on Melville's story, "The Paradise of the Bachelors and the Tartarus of the Maids." She talked about how Melville saw the plight of the worker in the machine age early on and how he showed the women workers as those sacrificed for the luxuries of the rich. Well I was taken with her bright green eyes and her keen intelligence and high spirit. She liked me too and we became lovers, but when I told her that I'd like to leave the road for good and marry her, she told me that she had no interest in marriage. Well, that was it, so I left and heard later that she had had my son. I went back and gave it another try but the answer was still no. She was a strange one, proud and stubborn, that Molly. It was not accepted to be a single mother in those days, not that it is now, but it was worse then. But she believed that marriage would take away her independence. "I belong to no man," she told me kindly.

So my son, Herman, grew up there and, later, in Louisiana where Llano moved. I would send him letters and get some back when he was growing up. Later they ended up back in Los Angeles and I got to visit him once or twice when he was a boy. A real great kid, he was. He left home real young too and got married to a fine girl. Unfortunately, he joined the army during the early days of World War II to go and fight the Nazis. He left his wife at home pregnant with my grandson, little Joey. So sad to think he never set eyes on his own son. That will set with me to my grave, I'll tell you.

I stopped dead, "Joey?" Now the mere coincidence of "Jack Wilson" just got a whole lot stranger. Joe was my father's name and what little I knew of my family history, one thing had always been etched in my memory—my dad never knew his dad who had "died in the war." I sat there for a moment shocked at the possibility that I really had stumbled onto my great grandfather. No, I thought, it couldn't be true. What are the odds? I read on with a stunned fascination.

Never got to see much of my grandson as my son's wife re-married quickly to another soldier boy who wasn't particularly interested in his stepson having a grandpa. I did write him a letter now and then and I got a few back with some pictures. It can be a lonely life rambling around like I have. But I don't regret much, what else could I have done? In fact, I'm proud I've lived to old age as a rebel, not somebody's yes man. And I'm proud my son died fighting Fascism. Maybe the revolution will come for the grandkid [laughs]. I can only hope.

Anti-War Speaking and Repression

After the free speech fights, the First World War came, and unlike the Second World War against Fascism, this was a war where the worker did not have a real stake in the fight. We were pawns in their game. Not all the Wobs were quick on the antiwar issue, but most were, I think. Well, I did some anti-war soapboxing in San Francisco and Los Angeles in 1917 and there were plenty of workers who were responsive to not getting their brains blown up in a fight between bosses. I always believed that there wouldn't be no war at all if it wasn't for the competition for resources that capitalism creates. Really, nations and nationalism is all a bunch of made up stuff. It's the same with races. We're all just humans and the divisions between us have all been created to serve the interests of those at the top who benefit from a divided working class. There is that famous line about one of the robber barons telling his fellow parasites that he could hire one half of the working class to kill the other half. Well that's how I saw it. Other than the war to defeat Fascism, I can't think of a war that's done any good—even World War II was used by the rich to make plenty of profit on arms and materials to fight the war. And what happened after WWII? They invented the Cold War to keep the machine rolling on. They've always got to have an enemy to distract folks with. Otherwise, we might point the guns the wrong way, as the old Pete Seeger song says—at them.

Well, back during the Great War, the bosses used the whole war hysteria very effectively to crush the I.W.W. All of a sudden we weren't against the bosses we were against "Americanism," whatever the hell that was or is. Hell, they got folks so riled up they had to rename the frankfurter "the hot dog" so folks didn't have to feel like they was supporting the Kaiser when they ate a sausage. It was ridiculous as hell but it worked. They passed the anti-syndicalism laws that pretty much made it illegal to be a Wobbly. So if you had the little red card, you were an outlaw. Within the I.W.W. there was a big debate between the folks like Elizabeth Gurley Flynn who wanted the Wobs to evade arrest and fight the charges and the folks like Big Bill Haywood who wanted to fill the jails. "We're in here for you; you are out there for us" was the slogan. Those in the Haywood camp felt that there would be a big wave of working class support for the prisoners, but it never did happen that way. When Haywood left the country that caused a lot of bitterness amongst the Wobs, who felt betrayed. I have to admit, I was with the Flynn crowd. After some of the treatment I saw myself during the free speech fights, I just couldn't see the point in handing myself over to rot in jail. It ruined a lot of people, those long sentences. And the organization was never quite as strong after that.

Some writers I've read say we disappeared. That's not true, but it is fair to say we were never the same. And other folks talk about how the McCarthy hearings and such were the only red scare, as if the Palmer Raids and the war on the Wobs never happened. It's my opinion that the second round was a picnic compared to what we faced, but that's neither here nor there.

So when a lot of the boys were getting rounded up, I took off and laid low. I got a job washing dishes on a ship out of San Francisco and there were a few other Wobs in my situation that did the same thing. A lot of the sailors were old Wobs and that was evident later in the city during the big general strike in the thirties. Lots of us old Wobs stayed around in labor circles and served as a resource or did organizing ourselves. When you think about the great sit-down strikes and the general strikes of the thirties, it wasn't anything else but sabotage—the conscious withdrawal of efficiency. I ended up with the Longshoremen under Harry Bridges for a while, but I do admit I had a few periods where I fell into the bottle and disappeared into the Tenderloin for a patch or two. It turns out that it was an old Wob who remembered me that dragged my ass out of a flophouse for the last time. He was running a little bookstore and gave me this job here in this shop. I have to admit selling paperbacks after years of bustin' my behind was quite a relief. So here I am.

I looked at Pete who had fallen asleep over his book. His feet were up on the desk and his book was resting on his chest. I kept at it:

Legacy

What's the legacy of the I.W.W.? I think that we had the idea that everybody was a human being. That was our radical idea—that there's nobody who doesn't deserve a piece of the pie. I know, in my case, the I.W.W. gave me a purpose, a channel for my anger, and a sense of pride that I mattered in the world. I know lots of other folks might have a more philosophical response, but for me, the basics are what matter most. We were the first to insist that there was no aristocracy in labor—that the unskilled and the skilled, black and white, immigrant and native, men and women all belonged in the One Big Union. There would have been no CIO without us and we were fighting for the rights of all workers before the Civil Rights movement. We believed in workplace democracy before anybody else, and something else—we had a hell of a time. We weren't too serious to laugh or too high minded to enjoy ourselves. And we had ourselves one hell of a life, one hell of an adventure.

I remember standing by the rail of a big steamer I was on, looking out at the moon over the Pacific and thinking that there wasn't a place in the world where I wouldn't be at home. Anywhere where there were workers with a fight, anywhere where folks were getting together. We had that sense, that we had no homes but the whole world was our home. Many of us had no family to speak of but every man was our brother, every woman our sister. It was a beautiful moment. Even if we took our lumps, it was worth trying. What the hell are you alive for if you don't even try? We had nothing, but we had everything. Understand? It's hard for me to put it into words really. Lots of folks today just can't understand the feeling we had. I don't know what else to say really. I lived the way I lived and I'll die that way—with nothing and everything.

And that was it, the end of his story. I looked over and Pete was still sleeping so I sat back and tried to grok the possibility that I may have actually discovered my great grandfather. Even if I hadn't, it was an incredible story from start to finish. I could do a book with this much material. Neville would jump on this for sure, I thought. It was getting dark as I got up to give the materials back. I touched Pete gently on the shoulder to wake him and told him what I thought I was on to. When I asked him if he knew anything about the author of the manuscript, he smiled and told me to sit down by his desk while he got a cup of burnt smelling coffee from a pot that had been sitting there all day. He offered me some and I accepted, taking a white styrofoam cup from his hand. Pete took a sip and said, "I did the interview, son."

"You knew Bobby Flash?" I asked, amazed.

"Not well, but yes. I was doing a project on local labor history for the Labor Council's oral history project when I was just getting involved. When I started interviewing some of the old timers I found out that a lot of the guys who'd been on the waterfront and involved in the General Strike had started out as Wobblies. I finished collecting the interviews for the council and then I thought I'd do a book on the old Wobs as a separate project, to honor them mostly. I got about half done and then so many of them started dying that I lost the chance to record them all. I still thought the interviews that I did have were valuable but I could never get a publisher, so there you have it."

"How did you find Bobby?" I asked, fishing for anything else I could get from Pete.

"I hooked up with him through one of the other fellows who met him at the bookstore in the Tenderloin. It was owned by an old Wobbly, the one who got Bobby off the streets and into a rehab program. Then he gave him a job in the shop. Bobby had that job until he died, sometime in the early sixties, I think it was. It's gone now. Shut down after Montana Slim, the owner, died not long after Bobby. There was a whole network of old lefties up here, still is, for now. Once the waterfront industries dried up, it got more diffuse, but there are still a number of us around who knew the old guys." Pete looked wistful about the good old days. I was desperate for some information that could confirm or deny my relation to Bobby, so I kept pressing.

"Anybody who knew Bobby well?" I probed further.

"Not anymore, I'm sorry to say. I wish I could send you to someone who had more for you, but the boys who were close to Bobby are all gone now."

"That's frustrating," I said, clearly disappointed. Pete looked at me sadly. Then, out of the blue, he lit up.

"I just remembered something, don't ask me how, but when Bobby died, I recall helping Montana go through his things in his room. It was a little place and he didn't have much, but I'm pretty sure that Montana sent a package of his things to an address in Los Angeles. It was his grandson's folks I think. Maybe your family would have it somewhere—if your theory is right, that is. For now, why don't you keep the manuscript? If Bobby was your great grandfather, you should have it. Just let me know what you find out, OK?" I shook Pete's hand, thanked him for everything, and promised I'd let him know the end of the story. As I was making my way downstairs he stopped me.

"You know, I might have another thing or two now that I think of it. I'll have to look through some things at home. I can't guarantee it, but I might still have something else. Where are you staying?" I gave him the name of my motel in Chinatown, near North Beach, along with my room number and tossed in my home address for good measure, before I finally hit the street.

Outside it was dark and the cold air was bracing. I had promised Shane I'd meet him for a beer before I flew down to San Diego the next day, so I looked for a payphone, but couldn't find one on the street, even after walking for several blocks. Nobody used them anymore so it didn't make sense to keep them on the street. Unfortunately, I was the last man in the world without a cell phone. I walked into a little bar with an old neon "Cocktails" sign, only to find that someone had ripped the world's last payphone off the wall. The barkeep was nice enough to let me use the phone behind the bar. I left a message on Shane's cell, ordered a beer and sat down alone in a booth in the corner.

My mom had cut off all contact with Dad's side of the family, so no one would have ever had the opportunity to tell me any stories about my great grandfather. I'd have to find my grandmother somehow. The last I'd heard she was still in LA somewhere, but that was years ago, when I was a kid getting birthday cards from a grandmother I never saw. Sandy had gotten into some fight with her about something soon after that and I stopped even getting cards. I looked at the row of gray and white heads drinking at the bar and wondered if they were somebody else's lost father or grandfather. I wondered if I had any other family I'd never met in California, Mexico, or somewhere in a distant port where a bold Wobbly seaman had met a fine girl.

9

The next morning I woke up and saw that the light on the phone next to my bed was flashing. I hadn't noticed it, but it had been late and I'd ended up getting pretty drunk with some crazy woman named Tanya, whom I met at the Saloon in North Beach after Shane blew me off to have a reunion with an old flame. I had thought I was getting lucky too until Tanya's boyfriend, a psycho biker in Hell's Angels colors, showed up and did shots with us, while eyeing me suspiciously every time Tanya gave me a sideways glance. It was an invitation for trouble, so I beat a hasty retreat and stumbled into bed without even thinking I might have a message.

It turned out that it was Pete. He'd dug through his things and hit the mother lode it appeared. He sounded excited. I checked the clock. It was 10:00 AM and my plane left at 1:30, so I had time. After I took a leak and splashed some water on my face, I called Pete's number. When I spoke to him he told me that the People's Archive was closed on Sunday, but he'd be happy to have me over to his house in Bernal Heights. I got the address, hurriedly showered, jammed my backpack full of my things, checked out, and walked a couple of blocks to Café Trieste for large cup of coffee to go. As I stood in line, I closed my eyes and listened to the Charles Mingus album they were playing. A couple at the table by the front door were debating the merits of Obama's foreign policy. Outside, I laughed as a chopper rolled by, fortunately not driven by the jealous biker from the bar the night before.

Coffee in hand, I hailed a cab out on Columbus. The driver was a sullen Russian with no social graces. He raced across the city efficiently, however, and we were headed up a big hill to Pete's house in Bernal Heights in no time. I checked the address, paid, and hopped out without even receiving a nod. The house was a large, shabby Victorian that had clearly missed the gentrification memo. The paint was worn down to the bare wood in places, and it looked as if it hadn't been cleaned up in years. Still, it was a great old place. Pete met me at the door with a hearty handshake. The living room was a stunning mess with piles of newspapers, books, and mail occupying nearly every open space. The walls were covered with old posters ranging from reproductions of Wobbly stuff and ILWU strike flyers to some sixties concert posters from the Fillmore. I stopped to look at a Grateful Dead poster from 1967.

"You see that show?" I asked.

"Yup," Pete replied nonchalantly. "You might be even more interested in some of these," he said gesturing toward the hallway that led to the kitchen. It was lined with framed original I.W.W. newspapers and posters.

"Take a look and I'll make us some tea." I nodded and glanced at the cover of the program for the Pageant of the Paterson Strikers. The central image was that of a worker climbing over a factory with arms outstretched. "Performed by the Strikers Themselves," it announced of the grand event to be held at Madison Square Garden. There was a newspaper headline in *Solidarity* proclaiming "Industrial Freedom" accompanied by an image of a woman in a flowing gown walking out of her chains and into a glorious sunrise. As I continued on, I looked over into the bedroom, which was in a state of genteel squalor similar to the living room. Underneath the smell of the brewing tea, the odor of years of dust was thick and pervasive.

"Fellow Workers: Remember! We are in Here For YOU; You are Out There FOR US." was the caption that I remembered from Bobby's interview. Here, it was accompanied by the image of a stern Wobbly pointing at the viewer from behind prison bars. Another poster displayed the skeletons of "justice" and the "judiciary" about to be buried by a mound of "capitalism." These hung next to a series of funny cartoons featuring "Mr. Block," with his big square head, being duped by his bosses and the media. The last one was an immaculately preserved cover for the sheet music for "Rebel Girl" by Joe Hill. On the wall across from the Wobbly stuff, Pete had hung a bunch of thirties labor posters and papers. The place was like a museum, where the order and cleanliness of everything else in the house had been sacrificed to the preservation of labor history. The frames alone must have put Pete out quite a bit. I wondered how he could have afforded to buy such rare pieces of the radical past.

"Where'd you get all these?" I asked intrigued.

"Dead Wobblies," he shouted from the kitchen. "Lots of those old guys didn't have any family to speak of. They knew I'd take care of them." Pete walked out with two cups of tea in mugs that bore the stains of many years. Well used, but clean.

"Let's start in the backroom," Pete said as he led me down the hallway to a small room occupied by another mountain of periodicals and a wall of cardboard boxes. I glanced outside the window and noted some rusty metal lawn chairs scattered in his unkempt yard, full of tall grass and weeds. The sun was breaking through the clouds, and a ray of light lit up the room for a moment before another cloud cut it off again. Pete picked up one of the shoeboxes and motioned for me to sit down with him in front of an ancient, pock-marked wooden desk where he laid out a series of old black-and-white photos. They were all group photos of I.W.W. members. One was a group at the Chicago headquarters standing behind Emma Goldman and Ben Reitman.

"That's Flash," Pete said pointing to a face in the back row. I looked and nodded.

"Sure looks like it," I said before glancing at another shot of Elizabeth Gurley Flynn posing in front of a Wobbly storefront with Flash in the first row, the second man to her right.

"Where's that?" I asked.

"Not sure," Pete said. "Look at this." Here was a shot of Mother Jones speaking to a group of workers in a tent camp. "Might be Ludlow, Colorado. Can't be sure, but there's Flash again." It was astonishing. I stared hard at the photo and shook my head.

"Christ, he was like a Wobbly Zelig. Did he ever talk about these people with you? I didn't see anything in the interview, but there were pages missing."

"Yup, I know," Pete said, looking a little sheepish. "As you can see, I bit off a little more than I could chew. The answer is yes, I think he did mention it in other interviews that I didn't transcribe—a lot of the old fellows had been all over the place. I used to have the tapes but they got damaged. A lot of this stuff I gave up on once I couldn't get a publisher. I just kept thinking I'd do something with it, but I never did. Now even my memory isn't that great. But once you left the other day some things came back to me." He put the photos in a manila envelope from the floor and handed it to me.

"Now let's head down to the basement. There's more." I stood up and followed Pete down some rickety stairs into the dark until he found the light switch. After I was done blinking, I was astounded to see the walls lined with shelves stuffed full of cardboard boxes. On the floor there was a row of steamer trunks. Pete made his way over to one and opened the lid to dig around.

"What is all this?" I asked, feeling as if I had stumbled into some kind of Hardy Boys mystery.

"Personal effects," Pete said. "The old boys didn't just leave me their posters." He dug through a stack of tattered trousers and shirts until he found a wooden box with a small lock on it. Pete turned it upside down and grabbed the key that was taped on to the bottom. He put the key in the lock, opened the box, and grinned at me as he held up what appeared to be a small vial.

"This is a tiny bit of Joe Hill's ashes, at least that's what Bobby used to say. Lots of the Wobs who were around back in the day claimed to have some." I remembered reading how Joe Hill, the famous Wobbly bard, had been framed for murder and executed in Utah in 1914. His body was sent to Chicago where it was cremated, and his ashes were mailed to every I.W.W. Local. An envelope full of them had been seized by the US Postal Service back in 1917 and held at the National Archives. The I.W.W. finally got them back in the late eighties, and the last bits of Hill were scattered across the globe from Sweden to Nicaragua, to a cemetery serving as host to the remains of anonymous Wobbly coal miners killed in a strike.

"It's a religious relic almost," I said, "like a piece of their martyred saint."

"It was his most prized possession," Pete replied. "Keep it."

"Thank you, Pete." He nodded and reached back in the box and handed me a small stack of bound letters and a diary.

"These were his, too. Now they're yours." Finally, he took another ancient, plastic-wrapped photo from the box and handed it to me. It was a shot of Blanco and Flash with their arms around each other's shoulders in front of their horses. The picture was close to crumbling, so I gently turned it over and saw that Bobby had written "Brothers Forever" on the back.

"That's everything," Pete said with finality.

"It's amazing. I can't believe it's all his. Thank you, so much."

"Do me a favor. Tell the story. Pick it up where I left off and give it to the world," he said.

"I'll do my best," I replied. As we headed back up the stairs I glanced at the other steamer trucks and wondered what other mysteries they held. Up top, Pete bent over and brushed the dust from downstairs off his pants. I looked at a clock on the wall and saw that I only had an hour until my plane took off.

"Pete, I'm sorry, I have to go," I said apologetically. "I wish I could stay here and look this over with you, but I can't afford to book another flight."

"No problem, kid. The phone's over there if you want to call a cab."

I thanked him and picked up the phone. While I was on hold, I noticed that Pete was smiling. I got the sense that he was pleased to have been able to pass the torch to me. It made me wonder if he had really forgotten or if he had had a change of heart. When the dispatcher got back on the horn, she told me the cab would be there in five minutes, so we walked out front through Pete's shrine to lost history. Outside, the sun had struggled its way out. When the cab got there, I gave Pete a hug, which he returned heartily, and I was off to SFO.

When I got to the airport, I grabbed my boarding pass at the ticketing kiosk and was dismayed to find a long security check line. In line, I was struck by the dramatic contrast between the generic, antiseptic yet paranoid space of the airport and the dark, dusty antique chaos of Pete's house. When I got to the TSA agent, I showed him my boarding pass and ID, took off my shoes, and put them along with my backpack on the conveyor belt to be screened. I'd thrown away my tiny toothpaste, but I was suddenly panicked that they'd try to take the vial of ashes. On my way through the metal detector, I tried to show an external calm while I kept my eyes locked on my stuff. To my great relief, my tiny piece of Joe Hill snuck past Homeland Security unmolested, or so I thought, until the guard at the x-ray machine pointed at my backpack just as I was retrieving my shoes from the conveyor belt. Another screener grabbed my pack, unzipped it, and went straight for the little brown vial. After they took it out and looked it over, another guard came up behind me.

"Sir, please come with me," he said in a disconcertingly neutral tone. I noticed that the passengers in line were gawking at me as I followed the guard to secondary, which pissed me off.

"Please sit down, sir," the guard said. I did, struggling to control my tongue all the while.

"What is this about?" I asked as calmly as I could. "I'm going to miss my flight if you keep me here much longer." He ignored my question and asked me to stand and hold my arms out at my sides while he brushed yet another metal detector across my torso and up and down my legs. I had still not been able to put my shoes back on, so I offered to take my socks off so they could smell them.

"That won't be necessary, sir," the guard replied unfazed. He was a forgettable-looking fellow with short brown hair and a bland, tired expression.

"You can sit down now, sir."

Another guard, a stocky fellow with a pit bull face under a crew cut came out and motioned the other guard away.

"Are you carrying any illegal drugs with you, sir?" he barked.

"No. Is this about the vial?" I asked, unable to conceal a smirk.

"We're examining the contents, now," he continued brusquely. "You may as well tell the truth."

"Believe it or not, it's a bit of Joe Hill's ashes," I blurted out.

"That doesn't mean anything to me, sir," he said, without a hint of emotion. I paused, remembering that the Transportation Security Administration had been created as an explicitly non-union entity by the Bush Administration—all in the name of our safety, of course. Hence, this pit bull wouldn't know Joe Hill from a hill of beans.

"He was my grandfather," I lied. "He used to play football for the San Francisco 49ers back in the day, as a matter of fact. The family scattered most of his ashes at the old Kezar stadium, but we all kept a little bit of him for ourselves to remember Grandpa." This seemed to lighten him up a bit. He disappeared into the room where they had taken my backpack and were presumably examining Joe Hill with some high tech gadget. I doubted, however, that they could determine family lineage in the airport, so I was confident that my secret was safe. When he came back out, he was carrying a piece of paper with him. He handed it to me and told me it would be just a minute. I took a look at the paper with the US Department of Homeland Security seal, complete with the eagle, stamped on the top:

Transporting the Deceased

Traveling with Crematory Remains

We understand how painful losing a loved one is, and we respect anyone traveling with crematory remains. Passengers are allowed to carry a crematory container as part of their carry-on luggage, but the container must pass through the X-ray machine. If the container is made of material that generates an opaque image and prevents the security screener from clearly being able to see what is inside, then the container cannot be allowed through the security checkpoint.

Out of respect to the deceased and their family and friends, under no circumstances will a screener open the container even if the passenger requests this be done. Documentation from the funeral home is not sufficient to carry a container through security and onto a plane without screening.

You may transport the urn as checked baggage provided that it is successfully screened. We will screen the urn for explosive materials/devices using a variety of techniques; if cleared, it will be permitted as checked baggage only.

Crematory containers are made from many different types of materials, all with varying thickness. At present, we cannot state for certain whether your particular crematory container can successfully pass through an X-ray machine. However, we suggest that you purchase a temporary or permanent crematory container made of lighter weight material such as wood or plastic that can be successfully X-rayed. We will continue to work with funeral home associations to provide additional guidance in the future.

When I was finished, I shook my head in disbelief. It was utterly surreal, I thought. Finally, another guard came out and explained that the brown glass was somewhat opaque and that had made it difficult for the screener to determine the contents, since I had not disclosed that I was carrying crematory remains. Then he handed me back my carry on.

"I'm sorry for your loss, sir," he said, not particularly convincingly. "You're free to go." I was tempted to tell them they had just liberated an enemy of the state, but I said nothing, put my backpack under my arm, and ran to the gate just in time to catch my plane. I was the last one on and had to sit in the back, which was fine because I wanted to be alone to read my newfound treasures.

I buckled up and ignored the obligatory safety instructions. If we crash, we'll all die, I thought. On that bright little note, I opened the bundle of letters. As with the photo I'd seen at Pete's place, these old letters were well preserved, but fragile. The first one was from Gus Blanco sent from Everett, Washington to Bobby care of I.W.W. Headquarters in Los Angeles. It was post-marked November 1st, 1916:

Dear Bobby,

I just heard word from a comrade here in Everett that you survived the business in San Diego. My heart is filled with joy on the news, dear brother, as I had long feared you dead. Here in Everett, the situation is dire, but courage has not deserted us. If we could get out of Mexico in one piece and slip the noose in Holtville, why not dodge the vigilantes here in Everett? Remember what we said back in Coyote Well: "Better their horses under our asses than our asses in their noose"? This time, I'll not go down without a fight either brother. If you hear of me no longer, remember me to the future, my friend. If we make it out alive, we'll raise a glass to the One Big Union.

In Solidarity, Gus

So Blanco *did* get word that Flash had survived! And this was his last letter before he was killed—amazing. Bobby had kept it with him to the end, and told his story to the future. Here I was on an airplane flying over San Francisco Bay with it in my hands. I looked out the window at the city fading into the distance behind us and picked up another letter. This one was from Molly O'Conner, it was written in the late teens as well:

Dearest Bobby,

I received your letter and it filled me with fondness for the time we have spent together, but I also fear I may displease you, my love. I too remember your tender caresses that day in Llano. I too remember the music in the distance and the beauty of the trees moving gently in the breeze and vast blue sky above. I too was moved deeply by our moment together and hold it as a most precious part of my life. I do most surely love you as you love me... but my love cannot belong to one man alone as my love belongs to the world. When I say to you that no man can own me, it does not mean that I love no man or that your affections are not held dearly. It only means that I do not believe in marriage, a property contract that has kept women in bondage for ages. Surely, my love, you can see the difference between love and a legal contract. We are both involved in a struggle larger than ourselves and have given ourselves to it, heart and soul. It is to this that we owe our full selves more than anything else. So, no, Bobby, I cannot marry you. You will be welcomed back to my loving arms any time our paths may cross, and know in your heart that you have my love, even if you cannot possess me. I think of you every day with great affection and shall never forget you. Please do not hold any bitterness toward me—I could not bear it. Carry me with you in your heart forever, a comrade and lover.

With most tender love, Molly

So this was a response from Bobby's one great love, Molly O'Conner, my great grandmother if my suspicions proved true. I was struck by the mixture of formal language and longing. Abstract politics and regret perhaps, or fierce independence, or maybe both. Who could know? And how did this leave Bobby? Heartbroken? Humbled? Full of bitterness? Or did he respect her choice? In his interview, he didn't show anything but a kind of distant affection for a lost past. I looked out the window again and noticed that we'd gone above the clouds. I picked up another letter from Molly:

Dearest Bobby,

I write you with good news. Since the time of your last visit I have discovered that I am with child. I ask nothing of you. I find myself unexpectedly joyous at the news, however, and am making plans for the child's birth and infancy. I shall continue my teaching and political work, of course, and what could be more revolutionary than sowing the seeds of the future? If it is a girl I think Emma would be a fine name. If it is a boy, I would prefer Herman. What think you, my love? Please let me know.

> With most tender love, Molly

How would Bobby have taken that letter? I stared out at the clouds in wonder. The pilot announced that the plane had reached cruising altitude and we could take off our seat belts. I looked through the stack for another letter from Molly and there were none. What I did see was a handful of envelopes with her handwriting on them from Herman Wilson. The first one was a small child's drawing of a stick figure with a smiley face. At the bottom, in Molly's handwriting, it said. "To Papa. Love, Herman." There were two more letters like that separated by six months and then a year. Then, in the early twenties, the handwriting changed to that of a small child. It was a crude drawing of a baseball player with "To my Papa, the ball player, Love Herman" written at the bottom. Under that envelope there was one more in a young man's hand from the forties. It was from Herman:

Dear Father,

I know it has been a long time since you have heard from me. I am writing to let you know that I have joined the Army and will be shipping out in a few days. While I understand and respect your objections to war and the military, we both know that this is a war against Fascism. It is a fight we must not lose. I cannot in good conscience ignore the call to arms. If anything happens to me, know that I went to my death with honor and with great love for you in my heart. Though we have not been able to spend much time together, I have always held your communication with me dear and hold you in great regard.

Your Son, Herman

And that was it—the whole written record of Bobby's most intimate relationships, in a few fragile letters. What fascinated me were the gaps in communications. Had Bobby thrown some letters away in anger or grief? How did he learn of Herman's death in the war? What became of Molly after Llano? Perhaps the diary would answer some of these questions. I figured I had another forty minutes at least, so I moved on to it, a worn, black, leather-bound thing with a few pages ripped out in the beginning. I skimmed through the book and was dismayed that the pages weren't dated, but the first entry gave me a clue: "I did not have a drink today." I read a few more entries and noted that a lot of them started the same way. Some were simply that one declarative sentence and others were filled with fits of self-loathing. "My entire life has been a waste," read one. "Not a soul on the earth will mourn my passing," read another. It was grim stuff. This must have been written during the days just after Bobby had stopped drinking and begun to get his life back together. It was probably during the fifties or early sixties, but there were no references to the outside world, no dates. One page was entitled "Regrets" and had the following list:

Never stuck with a woman
Never tried to find Patricia
Never finding out if rumors of a son by her were true

Losing track of Molly
Missing Molly's funeral
Never being a proper father to Herman
Missing Herman's funeral
Never seeing grandson
Losing Gus's letters
Relapse after relapse
Being too weak
Being a fool
Stooping to begging
Stealing from a brother
Losing my self respect

This heartbreaking entry was followed by another one with more self-loathing, and the line, "I am a bum like they used to say to us. I am a bum, a nothing. No one will miss me when I'm gone." Here I noted a few more ripped pages and then the tone changed:

Moment of insight today. I began the meeting with the usual belly-aching and then I moved on to talking about how we Wobblies never won anything and only got our teeth kicked in, again and again, and Montana interrupted and said, "Being alive is winning." This stopped me cold and I sat up and thought, he's right, they never killed me, as hard as they tried. I began to weep at this thought. And he says, "Remember how they always told us we were bums, well, we *ain't* bums. Being proud to be alive is being a man. You are a man Bobby, a remarkable man. How many fellas have done what you've done? Who has shown the kind of bravery you've shown? When you fall down, you get up. Get up, brother!" At this we embraced and something changed inside of me. I felt myself coming back. Being alive *is* winning.

This was followed by a bunch of blank pages and then another entry without any of the stuff about drinking or meetings:

> I have begun speaking to a young fellow about my life. He is putting together a history. Montana has gotten together a number of us and we are serving as what he calls, "a living history." Also spoke to Montana about some personal matters. He is going to help me find my grandson. Montana says this will help me come full circle. It can be a form of personal redemption just as the interviews are a kind of social redemption. I can give myself to others as a way to find myself again. Have begun reading a lot. The job in the store gives me the time and a full library.

More blank pages after this, some with pen marks and doodles, but no entries. Then another brief one:

> I have begun speaking at union halls on I.W.W. history. Montana calls it "planting seeds." Here's to hoping they keep growing when we're gone. We have found my grandson's address, which fills me with great joy. Now, the letter!

So this was how he found my father! I was almost certain of it now. I looked ahead eagerly for something about their meeting and there was nothing but blank pages, with a few more ripped out. Finally, in the middle of the empty pages, I found something, but it wasn't about my Dad:

> Went to the doctor today and found out that I'm going to die. I AM GOING TO DIE. Well, there it is, in bold on the page. What have I done with this life? If I had had to answer that question a while back, I wouldn't have had much good to say, but now, I feel I've done a little something, planted a seed or two. I only regret having not gotten to spend more than a

few visits with my grandson, but I'm grateful to have found him. Now, one last letter.

To the future, Bobby Flash

Strangely, a tear fell down my face as I leafed through the diary for more, but that was the final entry. I noticed that the man across the aisle was staring at me so I turned my face toward the window to gaze at the topography below. The pilot told us we were beginning our descent. I could have cared less.

10

On Monday I got into the office early, eager to talk to Neville and pitch my Bobby Flash story again. When I got there, Neville wasn't in but I did see our music writer and a group of freelancers huddling around a desk in the back of the office. I could tell by their mood that the news wasn't good, and I quickly found out that several of their paychecks had bounced and that Neville had been MIA all weekend. This gave me a sick feeling, but I stupidly said, "Neville's always been up front with me. I'm sure this is just some kind of mix-up." That got a collective sneer so I walked back over to my desk and found a note from Neville. He wanted me to cover a big protest at City Hall today. I grabbed my satchel and took off, leaving the gossiping writers to mull our impending doom. Perhaps it was my enthusiasm about my Bobby Flash discovery that did it, but I still wanted to give Neville the benefit of the doubt. He *had* always been straight with me and I didn't want to believe he could be getting close to going bust without letting us know.

When I got to City Hall, I could tell something big was going down. There were hundreds of picketers out in front of the building, chanting and yelling slogans over megaphones. One of the first things that caught my attention was a huge caricature of Frank Antonelli, the most conservative member of the City Council who'd made it his business to go after all the city workers. He'd been a vocal right-wing agitator for years before he ran for office. He directed a think tank called the Efficiency Roundtable, and his reports all had catchy names like "Pigs at the Trough: The Public Sector Union Bosses' Assault on Taxpayers." He was loved by the editorial board of the *Imperial Sun* and loathed by local unions. Antonelli had endeared himself to the local gay community by splitting with the Republican Party and supporting gay marriage, but many thought the move was a Machiavellian maneuver to split the progressive community on the eve of the outsourcing vote. He'd also infuriated local environmentalists by proposing that the city end its recycling program or at least outsource it. Antonelli's biggest support base came from the local Chamber of Commerce, which loved his unyielding opposition to all taxes. Hence, it was not much of a surprise that he'd been investigated for tax evasion. His brand of libertarianism was a variety of corporate anarchism—opposed to the very notion of government itself. He was contemptuous of public sector workers and considered them to be a species of life somewhere near the bottom of the food chain. Anybody who couldn't or didn't want to sell themselves on the market was suspect—a parasite in his view. Antonelli presented himself as a kind of reformer though, not the zealot he actually was. Much to the evil delight of his adversaries, he looked like a wet rat with bad hair plugs. When he smiled, it was impossible for him to conceal a kind of gleeful disdain. It just oozed out of him.

"Put Frank in the Tank for Tax Evasion," read one of the protest signs held by a member of the City Workers United. The protest was in response to Antonelli's proposal to privatize the city's trash collection, janitorial, and park maintenance services. The move would put hundreds of people out of work and would replace them with workers who made a third less money and had no health benefits. "Stop the Race to The Bottom," read another sign. I went over and interviewed a stocky sanitation worker named Omar who'd been with the city for over twenty years and who was just a year away from retirement. "This is a slap in the face," he told me. "That son of a bitch Antonelli is trying to turn every well-paying job in this city into shit work." I interviewed a middle-aged janitor, Carmelita, who wondered aloud how she'd pay for her kids' health benefits without her job. A gardener who worked in Balboa Park spoke to me about the care he put into the big flower displays every spring. "We care about our city," he said firmly. "Put that in the paper."

Inside the building, I went through the metal detector and got a seat in the back of the hall. They had to move the hearing to Golden Hall to accommodate the number of people who wanted to speak to the issue. And they lined up and spoke for hours. Antonelli's supporters were in fine form, assailing inefficiency and corruption and greedy, overpaid city workers. The councilman applauded them all and assailed the "union bosses." I thought about the way Bobby Flash talked about the bosses and shook my head. He would think this was an upside down world, and it was. The supporters of the privatization move were greatly outnumbered by the city workers and their supporters—family members, clergy, local progressives, etc. I recognized all the usual suspects on both sides. The stories of the workers were emotional, and it was grueling to sit and watch them pour their hearts out for hours, deep into the evening. The overall feeling one got was a sense of betrayal and humiliation underneath the anger. These were people who'd been proud of their work and now they were reduced to begging—literally—for their livelihoods.

Antonelli smirked and sneered throughout the proceedings, relentlessly keeping the speakers to their allotted time. The workers' supporters on the council snarled back at him. One of them was actually crying as she listened to a woman plead with them not to "destroy her future." Here, Antonelli interjected, "I'm concerned about the taxpayers' future. We're not in the business of providing jobs above market rate or paying for people's health benefits. We've been doing that for too long and someone needs to weep for the taxpayers." This got boos and hisses from the assembled throng along with a "hear hear" from the Chamber of Commerce crowd across the way. Two men got into a fistfight after a speaker on Antonelli's side called the union workers "communists sucking at the government teat." One of the workers, a Vietnam veteran, took offense and it was off to the races from there. Finally, after hours of public comment, the council passed the privatization proposal by one vote. One of the democrats turned his vote on the basis of the "undeniable savings to the taxpayers." After the vote, the place went crazy and they had to threaten to clear the room. I saw lots of the workers in tears and others sitting glumly staring bullets at the council. Some of the Antonelli supporters were high-fiving each other on the other side of the hall. I thought about Bobby Flash's talk about dignity and fighting back. It was a bad night.

When I left, Antonelli was being interviewed by a TV news crew, crowing about his victory and telling them that this paved the way for pension reform, the next item on his agenda. On the way out, I wondered what it took for someone to get to a place where they could take such relish in wrecking hope. I couldn't help but think he and his gang were vigilantes in business suits, ridding the city of the very notion that working folks deserved anything more than what "the market would bear," as he put it. These respectable thugs wouldn't be happy until the last union was busted, the last government services turned over to Wal-Mart, and the very notion of "benefits" of any kind had been made obsolete. Antonelli and his crew made the city's few moderate conservatives look like Mr. Rogers, and they wanted to drive the moderates out of existence too—along with the unions. They were in love with the war of all against all, no compromise. I went back to the empty office and angrily pounded out my piece. "City to Working Folks: Drop Dead," I called it. Neville had never come in that day. Nobody had heard a word from him for three days now. I emailed the story to Neville and hoped he'd be able to run it. Who knew what was happening?

At home, I was greeted by a message from Shane on my answering machine. The collective had a new venture: an internet magazine. They wanted to focus on local, national, and international politics. The idea was to make connections between people's lives as workers and consumers and the larger world. How could we connect what we ate and wore with the lives of distant others? It all sounded a little vague to me and, after the carnage I'd just witnessed, painfully naïve. When I called back, he didn't pick up, so I left a cranky, ungenerous message about how I was skeptical about the financial viability of internet media. I made myself a can of chili for dinner and ate it with some old bread and a Dos Equis. The news had Antonelli's smug face on all five channels. I went to bed and slept with no dreams.

11

The next day, I woke up late and headed into the office to see if Neville was there. No luck. I sat at my desk for a moment and watched the music reporter—Vivian was her name—cleaning out her desk, taking the "fuck work" magnet off of the metal filing cabinet next to her work station and pulling down the Coachella poster on the wall.

"Giving up?" I said as she headed down the stairs.

"Good luck, Jack," she said. "You're alright."

"You too, Viv," I replied. "Hang in there." It didn't look good, but *I* still hadn't given up. When I turned on my computer there was an email from Neville. It said, "Great piece. Will run it next week. Will explain everything. Take a day or two. See you next Monday." I knew things were weird but I willed myself to be encouraged by the note. Then I looked down at my desk and there was an envelop with my name on it. It was my pay—in cash. Very strange, I thought as I counted it out. There was no note either. Well, at least for the moment, I was still employed, technically. I was being paid, right?

After I sat at my desk for a bit longer, I thought I would use my unexpected time off to follow up on my ever-changing family history. The uncertainty at the office and the horrible Antonelli story had distracted me for a bit, but now the potential enormity of my discovery hit me with full force. I decided I'd call Sandy on Neville's dime. When she picked up her voice was odd, husky as if she'd been crying.

"What's wrong, Mom?" I asked her.

"Nothing," she lied. "Why do you ask?" After a long period of annoying denials, she let loose the fact that her latest boyfriend had left and she didn't know what she was going to do. I spent about an hour bucking her up and was just about to give up on inquiring about the family stuff when she asked about my work. I told her what I'd discovered with no details spared and plenty of enthusiasm. When I was done there was silence for a long time and then I heard Sandy crying.

"Why are you crying now?" I asked, genuinely puzzled.

"I was so bad to you," she whimpered. "I just thought I could start over and give you a new life. Please don't hate me for it. Please don't," her voiced trailed off and I spent quite a while assuring her that I didn't hate her—I loved her and knew that life wasn't easy. It all seemed like empty words somehow though. Somewhere in the cold hard center of myself, I knew she was heading downhill and might never recover. I felt utterly helpless in the face of this bitter realization.

"It's all gonna be OK, Mom," I told her. "I love you and I'll always love you. You'll get over this. You'll find someone new."

"You're too good to me," she said. "But I'm an old woman now. I might just be out of chances. But that's enough about me." I assured her that she had plenty of life left and tried to see if she remembered anything about Dad's family. Nothing. She did, however, think she still had my grandmother's information somewhere.

"Let me go see if I can find that old number," she said dutifully. I listened as she dug around in a dresser drawer for five to ten minutes. I wasn't counting. Finally, after several, "are you still theres?" she found a phone number and an address for my grandmother in LA—Santa Monica, to be specific.

"Be careful with her," Sandy said. "She's a mean woman. At least she was. It's been years. Who knows if she's still at that address or even alive?"

"Thanks, Mom," I replied. "That's a nice thought." After I hung up, I took a minute to get myself together. Sandy was always a disaster, but somehow she kept at it. Who knows, maybe she'd find some rich old codger.

I dialed the number and, after many rings, a frail voice came on the line. I introduced myself to my long lost grandmother and told her my story. After a long pause, she told me how odd this was to hear from me now that I was a grown man. Maybe it was God, she wondered; it was like a miracle. I held my tongue about God, but told her I was pleased that she was happy to hear from me. I would love to come see her and talk in person.

"I just might have something for you," she said tentatively. "I'm sure I've got it somewhere still." The possibility that she had something from Bobby Flash made my heart race with anticipation. I couldn't quite believe it was true, but it appeared it was. I thanked her and asked when I could come get it. Anytime was fine, she said, she didn't go out much anymore.

I got off the 405 and drove down Santa Monica Boulevard and turned onto my grandmother's street a few blocks from the ocean. It was a nice old craftsman. I knocked and waited. It took her a long time to get to the door, but she answered smiling, leaning on a walker, and looked me up and down with wonder. I strolled into her living room and saw a picture of someone who had to be my grandfather in his army uniform set to head off to World War II. It was Herman. After he died, she'd remarried another soldier who'd been with her all her life until about ten years ago when he died. I looked at Mrs. Betty Johnson, formerly Mrs. Betty Wilson, daughter-in-law of Jack Wilson, AKA Bobby Flash. She had to be in her nineties. Her long white hair was in a neat bun, and as we sat down together on her couch, I looked at her rheumy hazel eyes and wondered what it would have been like to grow up with a grandmother. I started slowly and asked her why she and my mother had stopped speaking. Betty explained that she and Sandy had never seen eye to eye. She blamed Sandy's leaving for my Dad's "getting into drugs"—that and the fact that Joe and her second husband, Mr. Johnson, had never had a good relationship.

"Being a military man, he expected more discipline than Joe ever had," she began. "Back in the sixties, when Joe grew his hair out and started roaming around the country, they fought horribly. Stanley, that was my second husband's name, used to say cruel things to him when he got angry. 'You're just a bum, like that bum of a grandfather you had. Do you want to end up like him?' Well, that really got to Joe because he'd gone to see his grandfather before he died and really held his memory precious as one might expect, but Stanley could be hard and he just expected Joe to follow orders. That was what he was used to, I suppose. Well, when your father died, Stanley felt responsible. It hit him hard and he wanted to maintain a relationship with you, to make up for it in some way perhaps. But Sandy wouldn't have it. She thought we were trying to take over. After a while, she wrote us and told us to stop writing you. We had a terrible fight and then she moved and we lost track of you all. I've always regretted it." I looked at her and her eyes were moist, so I put my hand on her shoulder, comfortingly, and said, "It's alright." Then she told me how Stanley had never liked Bobby because he thought he was a drunk and a communist. He'd fallen into the bottle up in San Francisco and, before that, he'd been involved in "terrible things." I looked over her shoulder and noticed that the Fox News Channel was on in the other room and repressed a smile.

"Anyway, Joe had looked up your great grandfather and gone to see him and he used to say things about what a great man he was. So it was a point of contention between us. I thought it was important for Joe to meet his grandfather, who'd stopped drinking by then, but Stanley didn't like it. He'd been the one who'd raised your father after your blood grandfather died in Europe when I was still pregnant with Joe and he thought your father was disrespecting him. So, Stanley felt betrayed. Maybe he felt like he was never really accepted as your Dad's father. We weren't able to have any children of our own, so I know it troubled him deeply."

I didn't care about Stanley, but I nodded along politely until she stopped herself and said, "But you came for this." Then she reached over to the end table by the couch, picked up a shoebox, and handed it to me. I opened it and found a picture of Bobby Flash standing in front of an I.W.W. headquarters with his arm around Gus Blanco. There was another of him as an old man with a big scruffy white beard, beaming from behind the counter at a bookstore. On the back of the first it said, "Your grandpa as a young man, solidarity forever!" The back of the second picture read, "Your grandpa as an old man, solidarity forever!" Underneath the pictures was Jack Wilson's little red card. Finally, I picked up an old letter addressed to Joe Wilson. I pulled out the yellowed paper, unfolded it carefully and read:

Dear Joey,

I am writing you this letter knowing that I won't be here when you read it. I went to the doctor a few weeks back and found out that I have cancer in my liver and not much time left. Before I go, I just wanted to tell you a few things. The first thing is for you to know that you had a grandpa who was proud that he had such a fine young man as a grandson. I only got to meet you a few times, but that was enough for me to know that you are destined to do great things in the world. As one of my favorite poems says, "Be a bold swimmer." Don't let them make you dream contemptible dreams. Do what the poem says, "Wash the gum from your eyes" and "habit your-self to the dazzle of the light and of every moment of your life." Never take shit from anybody, son. Life's too short for that. On your deathbed, you'll never be sorry that you stood up for yourself. Be kind to your comrades in need, and find a good woman when you can. Women are better than men, son. They are one of life's wonders. Never worry about how much money you've got. Home is everywhere, son. When you've got nothing you still own it all. It belongs to all of us. As I said, be kind to your comrades when they need it too. You never know when you'll need a hand yourself. And if you get lonely, remember, there I am in your blood, a little bit of old Jack will always be with you. In your heart and in your blood. Goodbye, my dear grandson.

With love and solidarity forever,
Your Grandpa, Jack Wilson, who some called Bobby Flash
because he got to the ball in time at short and the sidecar in
time in the yard

P.S. I have left a note for a friend to send you a few small things to remember me by. I hope they will find you well.

I looked up at my Grandmother, still amazed at what I had just read.

"Your father kept those things in the dresser drawer by his bedside," she told me. "You can keep them if you'd like to."

"I will," I said and thanked her. She asked me if I wanted to stay for some tea and I did.

"Let me make it," I told her. "Where's the kitchen?" She told me, and thanked me "for being so sweet." As we sat down with the tea, she asked what I had done with my life, so I told her my story, cleaned up a bit. It was the story of Jack Wilson, reporter, and his son Hank. When I took out my wallet and showed her his picture, she smiled with amazement at the first sight of her great grandson, all grown up. When I left, we hugged each other and I told her I would write her and let her know when she could meet Hank.

It was rush hour when I left, so I drove over to the Santa Monica Pier, parked the car in a lot nearby and walked down past the carnival games and the restaurants until I got to the end where I leaned on a rail above the ocean. I mulled over the letter that Bobby had sent my Dad, and the deathbed advice he gave him. Looking out at the Pacific glittering in the late-afternoon sun, the words came back to me. "Habit yourself to the dazzle of the light," I thought, "And every moment of your life."

12

Back in San Diego, things just kept getting weirder. I got into the office on Monday and it was empty. Neville was nowhere to be seen, but I noticed that copies of the *New Sun* were ready to hit the streets just as Neville had said in an email he sent me from his undisclosed location. I emailed him back and told him I thought I should start on the Wobbly piece on Bobby Flash. "My Great Grandfather, the Wobbly" I'd call it. I went down to a café on Fifth Avenue and ran into one of the part-timers, Matt, who helped with advertising. He'd gotten a second check, which was good. Most of the staff had split, but he too had gotten an email from Neville urging him to soldier on with no explanation. He did have one new bit of news for me, but it didn't bode well. We'd lost several advertisers who were cutting back on their budgets, and they were some of the biggies—weekly ads that catered to the La Jolla opera crowd. I held out hope that my Bobby Flash piece might live to see the light of day if we could squeeze out a final issue. It would be my San Diego swan song. Then, who knew?

We finished our coffees and headed back up to the office together and, much to our surprise, Neville was there. He looked drawn and tired, like he'd been pulling all-nighters during finals weeks.

"Boys, we're done," he said without any lead in to cushion the blow.

"Motherfucker!" I said angrily, but before I could really lay into him, he stopped me.

"Listen, I know, you're right," he said. "This is terrible form, but I thought I could pull it off." Neville went on to explain that his "trust fund" had long since been exhausted and that he'd been trying to make a go of it as a "real" business for the last year. We'd been treading water for most of that period until he started losing accounts from the big advertisers. After a while, even the discount ad space had stopped selling. The big papers were taking a beating too, he noted. Apparently, he had spent the last few days trying to secure a loan to keep us afloat for another few months, but he couldn't get it. Now, Neville, like us, was broke and out of work.

"Welcome to the high life," I said slapping him on the back ruefully. Matt said something else, equally stupid, and we all went out for a beer. After Neville's confession, I felt oddly liberated. We talked about my Bobby Flash story and he said it sounded like a good book, but publishing was in the tank too. Neville thought he might try to get a teaching job, but full time jobs were hard to come by and he didn't have any experience. Matt said, "We're so fucked," and we all laughed a hearty death row kind of laugh. When we finished our beers, I shook hands with the guys and went back up to clear out my desk. It had been a good run.

I took the bus back up the hill in a daze, almost missing my stop. When I walked by the Turf Club, I thought about more drinking but decided against it. Back at my place, I was greeted by a message from Hank. It was bad news. Trisha had lost it and attacked Kurt with a frying pan in the kitchen one night. He got a bad cut and actually called the cops to file charges. Trisha had moved out, into her Mom's place, and Hank was living on a friend's couch. I had a laugh at the thought of Kurt getting KO'd by a frying pan like a character in an old Warner Brothers cartoon, but I knew this was bad. When I called Hank's cell, he confessed that he'd dropped all of his classes so he could work more hours at his latest coffee house job. We went back and forth about this, but it ended with my inviting him to come down and visit. He agreed to come. I didn't have the heart to tell him about my new life as an unemployed journalist, nor did I think it was a good time to tell him about his newfound heritage. That could wait for later. Lacking a good way to avoid my own situation, I got off the phone abruptly, but felt bad about it.

Once I was off the phone, I changed my mind about drinking, grabbed a Stone out of the fridge and sat on the porch to think. My options in San Diego were pretty limited and I didn't have contacts in LA anymore. The big papers wouldn't touch a guy like me, and I had no degree and no other skills. Things weren't exactly coming up roses for me on the porch. I took a sip of my beer and watched a pick-up with a Raiders shield on the back window drive by with the stereo blasting Rage Against the Machine. It made me think of Shane and the job offer for the internet magazine. Maybe that wouldn't be such a bad gig after all. I took another sip of beer and gazed at a red Mini Cooper rolling by with the local news on. The radio said, "Frank Antonelli announced plans today..." before it faded into the distance.

I finished my beer and got up to call Shane to see if the job was still available and find out if they might have some work for a restless twentysomething with no degree or experience in the "collective" field. When I made my pitch, Shane laughed and said he would see what he could do. He sounded excited and that cheered me up immensely.

Once I was off the phone with Shane, I decided to call Hank back and apologize for giving him the bum's rush.

"That's OK, Dad, I didn't notice. Is something wrong on your end?" he asked earnestly. This led to a long pause before I bit the bullet and confessed.

"Well, I did lose my job today."

"Shit, you're kidding?" he said, clearly taken aback.

"Nope, I'm afraid not, kid. But I do have some good news for you—and a proposition."

"What? What is it?" he asked, excitedly.

"It's a surprise," I said. "It'll have to wait until I see you."

"You suck," he joked.

"I know. Talk to you later." I hung up, hoping that Hank wouldn't be disappointed with my revelation about his great grandfather and my crazy-ass plan for his future. If he was, I didn't have much else to offer.

Hank came down within a few days and he helped me pack up my things. Then we went for a long walk to Balboa Park. As we hiked down a canyon trail, I told him what I'd learned about Bobby Flash and he listened with rapt attention. After that, I filled him in about his great grandmother still being alive. He was intrigued. When we got to the Prado, we sat down next to a big fountain and I asked him if he'd be interested in living on the Lost Coast for a while. Without hesitating, he said, "Really?" like I'd just informed him he'd won the lottery. When I warned him it would probably be hard farm work or something like that, he still seemed fired up. There was a spark in his eye. It was the same look he had as a little boy when I told him we were going to a ballgame or Disneyland or some other cool place. I thought for a moment about how odd it was to only know your son through a series of episodes, always interrupted by a good patch of time. We'd never spent more than three days at a time together, but I still felt I knew something about the core of him—I was in his blood and in his heart. I decided I should show him Bobby Flash's letter to my dad when we got back.

It was a beautiful day, not a cloud in the sky, and we walked over to the sculpture garden for a sandwich, talking about what it might be like on the Lost Coast on the way. It was going to be our big adventure.

When we got back to my place, I took out the pictures of Bobby Flash, and showed Hank the letter. I'd never seen him look so serious. He read it and reread it. Once he'd finished with the letter, he picked the pictures back up and stared at them both for a long while. The look on his face was somewhere between wonder and disbelief. Finally, after he'd glanced back at the letter for a third time, he looked up briefly at me and then out the window nervously, at nothing in particular.

"How can you be sure it's actually from him?" he asked tentatively.

"Good question, I suppose. The writing on the back of the photos matches the letter, and the picture is certainly Bobby Flash too. Let me show you something else." I got up, took my satchel from my desk and dug out the mug shots, the print outs of the pictures I got from Wayne State, and the photos Pete gave me, along with Gus's, Molly's, and Herman's letters. After Hank took those, I passed him Bobby's diary. He looked them over carefully, for a long time, and nodded his head slowly as he compared the other pictures with the photos from Betty.

"Plus the timeline makes sense," I continued, once he was done. "And who the hell would take the time to make this shit up to fool a young man? What could be the motive? I know I don't have a birth certificate or anything, but I'm pretty damn sure."

"I didn't mean anything by it, I just..." he stopped himself and looked at me defensively.

"I didn't think you did, Hank," I assured him. "It's a trip, no?"

"It sure is," he said lightening up considerably. "Holy shit, my great great grandfather was a revolutionary and an outlaw!" Hank picked up Bobby's final letter again, reread it and looked up at me.

"What's the poem?"

"It's Walt Whitman, from 'Song of Myself.'" I walked over to my bookcase, grabbed a copy of *Leaves of Grass*, and opened it up to section 46. Hank took it from me and read it silently at first. When he was done, he looked back down and read part of it aloud, "Long enough have you dream'd contemptible dreams/Now I wash the gum from your eyes/You must habit yourself to the dazzle of the light and every moment of your life/Long have you timidly waded, holding a plank by the shore/Now I will you to be a bold swimmer/To jump off in the midst of the sea, rise again, nod to me, shout/And laughingly dash with your hair.'"

"Beautiful, no?" I said.

"Yeah," he said, nodding. "Fuck yeah."

I laughed and asked him if he wanted me to order some pizza, but he didn't answer. His head was back down, in the book, lost in thought. I let it go and just sat there across from him, for how long I don't know, watching my son read the poem that his great great grandfather, the Wobbly, would have hoped he would read after he was long dead.

To save money, Hank and I both sold our cars and combined the funds to get a used VW van. It seemed perfect, and we both joked about our new hippie wagon. We drove out of San Diego the day after we bought the van and stopped at Betty's house in Santa Monica. I stood and watched as she looked at Hank with the same sense of wonder that she had when she first looked at me. There were tears in her eyes and I could see that Hank was moved when she put her hand on the side of his face. We had tea and told her about our impending journey and new home and she thought it "sounded grand" that we would actually be together for the first time. After the visit with Betty, we grabbed the few things Hank had stored in the garage at Kurt's and got on the road again, stopping in Paso Robles for the night. We had dinner at the restaurant in the Paso Robles Inn before hitting the sack. When I asked Hank how long he thought he'd want to stay up north, he smiled and said, "Why don't we just get there first?" I let it rest. He was right, what was the point of trying to write the end of the story in the beginning?

The next day, we drove up through San Francisco and, after we crossed the Golden Gate Bridge, we decided to take the slow route up the Pacific Coast Highway. Hank had never seen the North Coast so he was enraptured with the scenery, staring off at the sea through the fog that clung to the hills like smoke on a fire. The luxuriant green coast and ragged cliffs made me think of Ireland. I put on *Astral Weeks* by Van Morrison and even sang along to a song or two. This was met with some friendly derision. The CD ended after what seemed like a million bends in the road, and it started to rain gently. We drove on for several hours without speaking, as the sound of rain lulled us into a meditative space. There was nobody else on the road but us for a while and it felt like we were heading to the end of the world. Finally, it began to get dark and we stopped at a cheap motel in Fort Bragg and slept like the dead.

In the morning the storm had passed, and the sky was clear and the air was crisp enough that we could see our breath. By the time Highway 1 hit 101, we were in the thick of Redwood country. I rolled down the window and breathed in the smell— dense and sweet. Hank was sitting beside me quietly, smiling. I passed a few logging trucks and put some Neil Young on the CD player, which seemed perfect. Hank nodded to me and we kept on, cruising through Garberville, Phillipsville, and Miranda before stopping for gas in Myers Flat as Shane had warned us to have a full tank for the drive to Petrolia. Once the tank was full, I called Shane on Hank's cell phone to let him know we were getting close, and we were on the road again. After we left Myers Flat, we hit the Humboldt Redwoods State Park in no time, turned off 101, and began our trip through the heart of the forest, down a steep switchback road to the Lost Coast Highway. Along the way, we saw a bear, a group of deer, and a myriad of blue jays flying above us. At the tiny town of Honeydew, Hank put on a Wilco CD and, when we hit the flat stretch that would take us to Shane's cabin, I found myself swept away by the beauty of the world. When the guitar solo on "Impossible Germany" began to soar in layers of ascending sound, I saw a hawk gliding above a golden field full of grazing cattle and felt as if I was deep into the texture of things, like we'd dived into a nineteenth-century landscape painting and taken up residence. It was—I feel dumb saying it—a moment of perfect grace.

Soon, we hit the tiny town of Petrolia and drove over a little bridge that crossed the Mattole River. We drove alongside the river for a few minutes until I saw a hand drawn sign that said "Welcome Jack and Hank." Here I turned down a long gravel driveway and saw Shane waving from the porch of his cabin. He greeted us and informed us that the other folks who lived near him were out for the day. It turns out that my fantasy of a big hippie commune in the woods was pretty crazy. In actuality, everybody in the collective had a place of their own. What they shared was labor and funds. Shane said he'd explain more later. For the time being, we hopped in the back of his pickup and drove down to the beach. We parked the truck in a little dirt lot and followed Shane as he led us along a sandy trail that hugged the green hillside by the ocean. The hills were covered with white Queen Anne's Lace, yellow tarweed, purple lupine, and orange poppies. We looked at the cows up on the hillside and stopped for a moment to watch some seals frolicking on the beach. Hank even spotted the tail fluke of a grey whale out on the water.

As we kept going, I noticed that we were the only people on the trail. We hiked on for a couple of miles and walked across a beach covered with pristine sea shells and a forest's worth of white-washed driftwood, before heading back up a hillside and turning down a path that brought us to a little cabin. We walked over and Shane opened it up. There were two cots on opposite sides of the cabin and a little desk with a couple of chairs. Shane told us that the only power came from solar panels on the roof and showed us to the outhouse in back. Then he walked back into the cabin and grabbed us each a beer he'd left with some ice in a big, old, metal cooler. We strolled out onto the front porch and sat down on the wooden steps. I took a deep breath of the salty air mixed with the scent of wild flowers. You could see a lighthouse in the distance. Hank told Shane that it was more beautiful than he could ever have imagined. We sat and talked about what the work would be like and I told Shane about the end of the Bobby Flash saga.

"You should write a book about it," Shane said.

"Who in the world would publish it?" I replied. Still, I was proud to be the heir of that legacy, no matter what the future held. It was late afternoon and the sun was getting low on the horizon, a golden road on the azure sea. I raised my beer and toasted us.

"Here we are," I said, appraising our humble new home, "in utopia." Hank and Shane laughed. It was going to be a hell of a time.

About the author

Jim Miller is the author of *Flash* and *Drift*, both novels. He is also co-author of the radical history of San Diego, *Under the Perfect Sun: The San Diego Tourists Never See* (with Mike Davis and Kelly Mayhew) and a cultural studies book on working class sports fandom, *Better to Reign in Hell: Inside the Raiders Fan Empire* (with Kelly Mayhew). Miller is also the editor of *Sunshine/ Noir: Writing from San Diego and Tijuana* and *Democracy in Education; Education for Democracy: An Oral History of the American Federation of Teachers, Local 1931*. He has published poetry, fiction, and non-fiction in a wide range of journals and other publications. Currently he teaches English and Labor Studies at San Diego City College. As a young man, Miller was a bouncer, a factory worker, a warehouseman, and a laborer in his late father's home repair business. A proud union member, Miller does political action work for his local. He lives in downtown San Diego with his wife, Kelly Mayhew, and their son, Walt.

Support AK Press!

AK Press is one of the world's largest and most productive anarchist publishing houses. We're entirely worker-run and

democratically managed. We operate without a corporate structure—no boss, no managers, no bullshit. We publish close to twenty books every year, and distribute thousands of other titles published by other like-minded independent presses from around the globe.

The Friends of AK program is a way that you can directly contribute to the continued existence of AK Press, and ensure that we're able to keep publishing great books just like this one! Friends pay a minimum of $25 per month, for a minimum three month period, into our publishing account. In return, Friends automatically receive (for the duration of their membership), as they appear, one free copy of every new AK Press title. They're also entitled to a 20% discount on everything featured in the AK Press Distribution catalog and on the website, on any and every order. You or your organization can even sponsor an entire book if you should so choose!

There's great stuff in the works—so sign up now to become a Friend of AK Press, and let the presses roll!

Won't you be our friend? Email friendsofak@akpress.org for more info, or visit the Friends of AK Press website: http://www.akpress.org/programs/friendsofak